CHOSEN

A LAST WITCH OF ROME NOVELLA

RHETT GERVAIS

Chosen
A Last Witch of Rome Novella

Rhett Gervais
Editor: Paula Grundy
Cover: Jake Caleb, J Caleb Design

Published July 2020
Copyright © 2020 Rhett Gervais

FOLLOW and LIKE:

https://rhettgervais.com/

PROLOGUE

A DAY AT THE MARKET

Antioch, the doorway to the exotic east and one of greatest cities in the Roman Empire. A mecca of trade where powerful merchant houses dealt in vast fortunes of silk and spice, where riches are made and lost in the blink of an eye... and today, it burned.

Thin shafts of sunlight cut through the smoke and haze, casting Antioch's market in a surreal light as Magda threaded her way through the chaos and destruction, all the while frowning at the dead and dying that lay in twisted heaps wherever she looked, their faces forever frozen in grim masks of death. It had been a warm day and the bustling market had been full of the sounds and smells of life. Vendors hawking their wares delivered that morning. Wicker baskets overflowing with fresh fruit piled high. Slabs of beef and lamb, just slaughtered, hanging in open stalls for shoppers to inspect, while meats of all kinds sizzled on spits, turning over white-hot charcoal, filling the air with the smoky, mouthwatering aroma of roasting flesh. Men and women in colorful clothing speaking, shouting, arguing, and laughing over one another in tongues familiar and foreign, while groups of street children in threadbare clothing raced around the adults or played underfoot. It was deathly silent now except for the lonely wail of an infant somewhere up ahead. Shifting her gaze to the world beyond the mundane, Magda winced at the vileness surrounding her. The weave here in the market was defiled and dim, faded like a tattered curtain too long exposed to the sun. The woman she was after had done this, violating the laws of nature so greatly that reality had struck back, bending and warping the world so where once there was a market full of life, now there was only death.

Beneath her feet the earth groaned, and she cursed when the aftershocks sent her stumbling and staggering along the debris-filled street. Catching her balance on an overturned table, she scanned ahead and found the veil of ash had cleared for a moment, long enough that she could just make out the shadow of the other woman, her target, snaking her way through the maze of burning tents and stalls. To Magda's amazement the flames never touched her, bending away from her like they were pushed back by some unseen wind whenever she approached.

Magda's first impulse was to lash out, use the flames to burn her to a crisp where she stood. It would have been easy under normal circumstances, but reality was fragile here, broken and twisted, and she dare not risk the child. Knowing that once the other woman was beyond the desecrated market, she would be free to use her power, Magda began a soft chant under her breath, tugging gently at the fragile weave, drinking in what little power she could without doing further damage, flooding her tired limbs with the strength of the stag and the deftness of the wolf. Next she reached out and shifted the debris around the other woman, sending a once colorful tent careening down in front of her. Subtle enough that it looked like a random occurrence, keeping the possibility of backlash to a minimum, but strong enough to send her stumbling to her knees so she could avoid being caught in the flames.

Grunting, she raced ahead with superhuman speed, bounding and leaping through the broken marketplace, her feet hardly touching the ground. In the time it took to draw a breath, Magda was blocking the woman's path, pressing a dagger against her pale throat. "Enough of this, Lillith," she said. "Look at what you've done, how far you've fallen."

Magda had expected her to deny it in some way, to rail against her, but the other woman said nothing, keeping her head bowed and speaking with a soft whisper, "You think I did all of this, Sister; you are sadly mistaken," said Lillith, looking up at her finally. Seeing her face, Magda recoiled in disgust, struck speechless by how twisted she had become. When they were children, her parents often joked that Magda was brilliant and wise beyond her years, and that Lillith was beautiful beyond measure. With her striking brown eyes and full lips and figure that was ripe beyond her years, it was true; she was breathtaking. But now her sister openly wore the scars of her many sins. Her once flawless dark skin was now a deep shade of blotted crimson, marred by welts and boils. Her smile, often praised in song by suitors from far and wide, was now a rotting grin, the stink of her breath making Magda gag in revulsion. Even the sacred runes that covered her flesh, the symbols of their people, of their power, had been turned into a mockery, the hieroglyphics replaced by a jumble of nonsensical white tattoos that twisted the eye.

"You have betrayed your oaths! And become the very monster that our people were sworn to defend against," said Magda.

"No, Sister! We have been lied to so that they may control us. We have so much power, yet we are taught to hold back, hide what we can do from the world," spat Lillith. "I have had a vision. We do not have to be servants to Rome. We can crush them! With our power, we can rebuild our empire to its ancient glory."

Despite the heat and flames surrounding them, Magda's blood ran cold. She had heard this before among the chosen, the desire to return to the old ways, that the Ose people had stood too long in Rome's shadow, and that they deserved to be more than just glorified servants and soldiers.

"Look around you, Sister. The old ways lead only to death and destruction. This is why we cannot expose our power to the world; reality strikes back, punishes us," she said, eyeing the squirming bundle in Lillith's hands. "The world has forgotten us: it is best that common man thinks we are little more than fairy tales. Our only hope for survival is to live in the shadows."

"Like vermin scurrying into dim corners, suckling at the teats of a corrupt empire, no, Sister, we deserve more. Join me and together we can remake the world as we want, a world where the Ose can rule once again."

Looking at the chaos around her, the dust and ash filling the air, the flames licking at her skin, and the reek of rotting flesh filling her nose, Magda shook her head. "No. I don't know how your heart has been corrupted like this, and I don't care. Just give me the child, and you can go off and get yourself killed in your mad quest. I won't bear witness to it."

Magda's breath caught in her throat when Lillith threw her head back and a raving mad cackle escaped her throat. For a moment she worried that the dark forces she conspired with had broken her mind, that the corruption had taken her, and that her mind was truly lost. With a burst of speed she lunged for the child, thinking it might be the only chance to save her, only to be blasted back by a gust of stinking wind that made her gag.

"No, Sister, you cannot have her. I've paid too high a price. Vesper and I have great plans for our people!" snapped Lillith, lucid once more.

"Vesper? You gave her a Roman name?" said Magda, sitting up.

Lillith scoffed, looking down at the child, with a rotting grin. "Vesper was an Ose name long before it was Roman! Don't you see, the empire stole our myths, our legends! They even stole the Loa, transforming such powerful creatures into their foolish pantheon. They are nothing but parasites!"

Magda shook her head in disbelief, amazed that her sister had fallen so far so fast. "There are too few of us left. She must be nurtured, protected so that our people can live on. I don't care that you're my blood, if you try to leave with her I will cut you down."

"No, Sister, she will be the end of our people. But I can stop—"

Without warning the earth heaved once more, and a violent tremor threw them both off balance and tumbling hard to the ground. Magda landed on her back, the wind blasted from her lungs. Part of her just wanted to lay there on the cool stones and catch her breath, let the pain fade away, but the pitiful wails coming from the child forced her to action. Blinking away the dark spots dancing in the corners of her eyes, she rolled to her side just in time to see Lillith scrambling on her hands and knees toward the screaming baby who had tumbled a few feet away, a frantic look of desperation on her twisted face. With the power of the weave still pulsing through her, Magda was faster, moving viper quick and reaching the child first, scooping it up one handed, and clutching it close to her breast.

"Give me the child or I will burn you where you stand," said Lillith, coming to her feet.

Magda turned, shielding the child with the body. "You would kill your own flesh and blood, for what, some mad dream? No, I don't think so, not after you have spent a lifetime standing against the dark."

"Are you are blind, Magda? Can't you see I am no longer the sister you led around by the nose. I have done things you can't imagine, seen things that would have sent you fleeing in horror. Don't think because we share the same blood that I will have trouble taking your life. I wouldn't hesitate, not even for a moment," she said in a voice so cold Magda took a step back, her brow creasing with worry.

She stared deep into her sister's unblinking eyes. Magda searched for any trace of the girl she made mud pies with when they were little, some sign of the young woman she teased incessantly after every boy in their village had proclaimed his love for her. She wished to catch a glimpse of her friend who would sneak out with her at night to gaze at the stars, dreaming of a brighter future, of how they would escape their tiny village and change the world. "The girl I knew is gone," whispered Magda at last, seeing only hate and rage in the other woman. "You truly are lost."

"Your eyes are open at last," said Lillith. "Now, give me the child. And for what we once were, I will let you leave in peace."

"No!" she seethed. "Never!"

"Very well, then," said Lillith, raising her hands and muttering an incantation in a tongue so vile it pained Magda's ear, her droning voice echoing across the burning market. In a panic Magda turned to run, adrenaline surging through her blood, praying that the strength and speed could take her beyond whatever horror Lillith was calling. She had managed a few feet when her way was suddenly blocked by a pillar of surging flames that licked at her hair and stung her skin. She pivoted to run back, and another pillar appeared just as quickly behind her, singeing the simple robes she wore. Clutching the child close to her chest, she sang in a loud, clear voice, desperately clawing on the ragged tatters of the weave, her piercing tenor drowning out Lillith's vile chant for a single moment, calling down a draft of cool air which washed over her, pushing back the scalding flames threatening to engulf her. Covering the child as best she could, she raced through the small opening in the flames, bounding like a gazelle fleeing the lion.

Looking past the broken cobblestones at her feet, she caught a brief glimpse of the edge of the market, and she pushed herself faster, hope giving her the strength to race on. Without warning she was yanked back violently by an invisible leash tearing at her throat, dragging her back with a jarring yelp. Magda clawed for a grip on the pavement, leaving bloody gashes on the stone as she was pulled back, using every bit of her strength to hold on to the baby, wincing in pain at the jagged stone digging into her soft flesh.

"You still don't understand," said Lillith, appearing above her, yanking hard at the invisible leash to silence her. "You think you can take what is mine! No, I will wipe the slate clean, burn away anyone and anything that stands against me."

Fighting to breathe, Magda could feel herself fading, the world going dark. Above her the light dimmed, like the sun had been eclipsed, leaving only pale shadows. "Lillith, don't!" she rasped, watching as her sister tore at the ragged threads of the weave, drawing torrents of power that rippled through her.

Lillith spread her arms wide, and a dark fog erupted from her, rolling over the market, snuffing out every trace of light. Despite the leash tugging at her neck, Magda managed to roll onto her belly, trying to protect the child from what was coming. All around her she was buffeted by a burning wind that sapped her strength and stung her flesh, pulling her apart bit by bit as though she were dust slowly being eroded, falling into nothingness. She opened her mouth to scream, to beg for mercy, but nothing came, only a hoarse whisper. Seeing all hope was lost, she curled up into a ball, the skin on her back and arms peeling away as it burned, her head pounding as if it were in a vice. From the corner of her eye, she watched Lillith weave her arms like a conductor guiding the orchestra to a full crescendo, her movements full of tightly controlled rage. A sharp wail pierced her ear, and with a start Magda realized that she was smothering the child. Using the last of her strength she shifted over, giving the small bundle room to see and breath.

Without warning, there was a choking gurgle from Lillith, the world going deathly silent when the vile chant spilling from Lillith's throat stopped. Magda looked up to find her sister standing stock still, frozen in place, staring at the child. At first she thought it was a trick of the light, but she swore she could see hints of emerald green shining through the blackness that dominated Lillith's dark eyes. But the longer she looked, the more her eyes changed, light and shadow dancing back and forth, like some battle being waged.

"I'm sorry, Magda," said Lillith in a strained voice that sounded more like the sister she remembered. "I only wanted to make the world better for our people, for her, but I was too weak."

Magda looked back at the child to see the same dynamic being played out in its unblinking eyes, dark shifting to light, green to gray. She shook her head in confusion, not sure what to do, when an ear-piercing scream exploded from Lillith's throat, her entire body trembling when the torrent of energy she was holding turned back on her.

The power ripping through her like a whirlwind of blades, gnashing and tearing at her hair and skin, leaving deep red gashes along her flesh. In a single moment her body and clothing were in tatters, looking like she'd aged a lifetime, bits and pieces of her flaking away and being carried off on the wind.

Magda reached out to touch her, to hold on to some part of her, but she blinked and her sister collapsed into a pile of dust, vanishing as though she never existed. Magda watched with awe while the dark clouds vanished, sunlight returning to the market, shining brightly as if nothing had happened. Feeling dumbfounded, she looked down at the child just in time to see the shadow fade from its eyes, leaving them green once more. The child smiled at her, and for a moment Magda felt a surge of hope. She would take it home and raise it as her own. The baby would never know what had happened, and given time, the world would forget too, just as it always had. She and the dead were the only witnesses and would tell no one. Magda would mourn her sister, but as always it was her duty to protect the legacy of the chosen, to keep their existence hidden, no matter the cost.

ONE

THE EVENING STAR

Vesper's first memory was of the great baobab tree that stood at the heart of her village. Even when the years of her childhood had long faded, she could still remember its towering height and wide branches, the feel of its rough bark under her palms as she climbed. Sometimes when she dreamed, she could still hear the rustle of wind blowing through its leaves. Throughout her travels far and wide, she had never seen another like it. Tall beyond measure, strong and unyielding, like her, like her people.

The earthy aroma of the forest always brought her back to her days clambering along the great tree's towering limbs and flowing branches, climbing so high that it seemed she could touch the sky if she just reached a little higher. And she had tried; she and the other children had always dared one another to greater heights, teasing and taunting as children do, but they were always stopped before things got too far out of hand. Her Aunt Magda was always there to keep them safe, seeming to be everywhere at once, shooing them back to the ground with a shake of her head and a knowing smile.

"How did you get up so high? I didn't even see you climbing," Magda asked one day after Vesper had almost fallen, her breath catching in her throat when her aunt grabbed her arm just before she slipped off a branch that was bending too far.

Her aunt's face split into a wide grin and she leaned over to whisper in Vesper's ear, "When you're ready," she promised with a wink. Then before she could open her mouth to speak, Vesper found herself on the ground far below, gaping up at the titanic tree, not remembering how she had gotten there.

At first it seemed perfectly normal; she imagined everyone could do such things, appearing and disappearing in the blink of an eye, but the looks of awe and wonder on the other children's faces told a different story. And Vesper and her friends spent many afternoons draped over the old tree's roots and branches, trying to puzzle out how her aunt managed to be everywhere at once. How she could be at the top of the tree one moment, and on the ground the next. But no matter how hard they tried to understand it, nothing made sense. Vesper had even tried to trick her more than once, pretending to be hurt, while the other children kept her distracted. She had spent the better part of an hour dangling off a branch, doing her best to appear like she was in danger, but her aunt never came. Worse still, when she returned home at the end of the day, her aunt gave her a knowing look, almost laughing at her.

Magda, her aunt, was larger than life to her, wise and knowing in all things. She was known far and wide in the province for making healing compounds and medicines for the sick, and while most of those who dealt in medicines sold little more than snake oil and false promises, her aunt was a true healer, an artist whose skills had saved more lives than she could count. From a young age, Vesper would spend her mornings running from one end of their village to the other, delivering her aunt's concoctions to the older folks in the village who couldn't get by without them or often enough to meet merchants who would deliver medicines to wealthy patrons in distant corners of the empire. Their community was a simple place, tucked away and forgotten in the northern corner of the Roman province of Africa Proconsularis, made up of freeman farmers, who spent their days under the hot sun growing golden wheat, and then came home to their small village at the end for safety and security. It was laid out in a circular pattern from the great tree, with most families living in small two-room cottages made from sod with thatched roofs, or in the case of a lucky few, like herself, a villa made of pale limestone covered by terra-cotta shingles. Her aunt's profession had the added benefit of surrounding their home with a marvelous garden that was the source of many of the plants she needed for her work. Vesper's father worked in Rome, and while he was absent for most of the year, his station, along with her aunt's medicines did afford them a better life than the common farmer.

"What was my mother like?" she asked one evening after they had finished their evening meal. They sat on a bench in the garden, gazing up at the star-filled heavens while her aunt braided her hair, her hands working diligently, deftly combing and twisting Vesper's hair so it lay flat against her skull in a complex series of braids, which kept her normally wild mane nice and neat. It was their favorite thing, to study the constellations and simply talk about their day, and they spent most of their evenings before bed doing so.

Magda's hands froze and she let out a deep sigh before speaking. "She was beautiful, and strong," said Magda, "A fierce protector of our people, so much so that even today our enemies speak of her in fearful whispers. And she loved you so much, and there was nothing she would not do for you."

"Until she got sick," said Vesper, repeating the story she was often told. Magda always spoke of her mother this way, as a hero, a larger-than-life titan, who protected her people and family but nothing more.

"Yes, until she got sick," said Magda, resuming her work with Vesper's hair.

"Yes, but what was she really like?" she blurted out, pushing her aunt's arm away and standing up, half of her hair sticking up in a wild Afro. "I mean, you've told me over and over that she was a great hero of our people, that she protected us. But I want to know real things.

Was she funny, or serious? What did she really look like? What was her favorite food, her favorite color?"

"What has brought on all these questions, child," said her aunt, finally looking at her, her brows coming together.

Vesper shook her head. "I run around the village every day. All the girls have their mothers... you know, to teach them how to be a woman, to just be with them. They—"

"You have me," said her aunt, looking hurt, dropping the comb in her lap. "Have I not done those things, taken care of you since you were hardly a babe... including that unruly mop you call hair."

"It's not the same!" said Vesper, starting to pace.

"Sit, child, calm yourself, please," said Magda, patting the bench beside her. "I will tell you what I can while we finish with your braids."

With a sigh, Vesper did what she was told, plopping back down on the bench and leaning up against her so that Magda could resume her work.

"When I said your mother was beautiful, I meant it. We were sisters, but no one would say that if they saw us together. She took the best from our parents. Our mother's high cheekbones and smooth, dark skin, and our father's height and strength and deep-brown eyes that could see into a man's soul, and often they did. When we were children, all the boys in the village pursued her, but she had eyes only for your father. Mostly because he didn't fawn over her like the others: that, and he could make her laugh."

"Really, Father is so serious now."

Her aunt gave her a wide smile, shaking her head. "He was much different back then. He was mischievous, a prankster, and he did everything he could to make her laugh; her laugh was infectious."

Vesper closed her eyes as her aunt spoke, leaning in closer, comforted by her warmth. "And was she really a hero?"

Her aunt hesitated before continuing, her voice low and calm. "Yes, our line has ever been protectors, tasked with keeping our people safe. She had a profound sense of justice, of right and wrong.

It wasn't enough for her to stop the spread of evil. She wanted to change the hearts and minds of all people that she met, all so that the world could be a better place."

"And did she?" asked Vesper, sighing deeply, her mind starting to drift, and her eyelids getting heavy.

"What?

"Make the world better," she said, closing her eyes.

"For a time," whispered Magda with a tremble in her voice. "For a time."

"Until she got sick?"

"Yes, she paid a terrible price for her efforts. We all did." Her aunt was silent for a long time, and Vesper came fully awake for a moment to find quiet tears rolling down, brightening Magda's eyes. She had never seen Magda cry and couldn't understand what could make her so sad. Her aunt had an iron will and often scoffed at the women in the village who showed emotion, calling them soft, weak. Not knowing what to do, Vesper wrapped her arms around the older woman's waist, burying her face into her side. "I'm sorry, Auntie. I didn't mean to make you sad. I won't ask anymore. I promise."

"No, child, you must always seek the truth; ask questions even if the answers are unpleasant. We must feel all of our feelings or we will become monsters."

"Yes but—"

"Enough Vesper, sleep. I will sing and watch over you."

Vesper nodded, placing her head on her lap. Magda began in a low voice, hardly a whisper. Singing an old song about a shango, a great Ose king who had been punished by God for his anger, forced to spend all eternity away from his family. Comforted by her aunt's warm embrace and soft rhythm, Vesper drifted off to sleep, dreaming of a woman with dark eyes and a warm smile like her aunt's, a woman she never knew, and would never know.

TWO

THE GIFT

Vesper never asked about her mother again. The hurt in her aunt's eyes was just too painful, but some of her words stuck in her mind, like an itch that couldn't be scratched. Vesper wondered what her mother did that made her so sick and how had everyone paid the price for it? She found out the truth not long after she had turned sixteen, and it changed her life forever.

"I heard some of the cooks talking about your aunt," whispered Aurelia, her eyes darting around to see who was listening. Aurelia was one of the girls Vesper grew up with, and she had grown more insufferable as she grew older. She was the first one of them to get her moon flow, and for some reason after that, she seemed to think it made her older and more mature despite them being the same age. She also had a deep love for anything sweet and often snuck about the communal kitchens trying to pilfer desserts, and as a result she picked up on most of the gossip that went around the village. Vesper never took much of what she said seriously; none of the children did.

She was a gossip on the best of days and took a special joy in the attention she got from spreading stories, stories that were often greatly exaggerated, or worse, often made up on the spot for attention. "They said she consorts with evil spirits, that she isn't really your kin, and she stole you from some poor merchant woman in the market," mumbled the small, hazel-eyed girl around a mouthful of sweet bread, all the while nodding like she herself had been present to witness Vesper's abduction. But on that day, something about what she said had a kernel of truth and it enraged her. Vesper didn't remember much after Aurelia had told everyone that her aunt was a servant of the underworld. All she knew was that one moment she was nodding along to what the other girl was saying and the next, Aurelia was launched through the air, flying like a bird, before landing on the dirt with a horrible crunch, clutching a bloody nose. Vesper could only remember screaming, "Liar!" over and over, her entire body trembling with rage.

Then, as always, her aunt was there, appearing from nowhere, and taking her into her arms. Vesper fought against Magda like a caged animal, battering and kicking while baring her teeth, but the older woman held her tight, rocking her back and forth while whispering soothing words into her ear until her blood cooled. With a shudder Vesper came to her senses and found that along with her aunt, a small crowd of parents gathered around the two girls, all of them staring wide-eyed and wringing their hands, faces creased with worry. She blinked in confusion for a moment until she saw Aurelia's face, bloodied and stained with tears.

"I told you the girl should not be here!" shouted a dark-haired woman with hazel-colored eyes that matched Aurelia's. "The girl is a savage just like her—"

"Mind your tongue, Gara!" snapped her Magda, her nostrils flaring at Aurelia's mother. "Or you will find out how savage I can be." The two women locked eyes, and Vesper felt like something passed between them.

Without another word, Gara took a step forward, standing protectively in front of her daughter who bowed her head, staring wide-eyed at Vesper from behind her mother's skirts. "No, Magda, I will not. Your family has only brought shame to our people, and I, for one, will not let my child suffer for your foolish pact. It was only a few cuts and bruises this time. What happens when she really hurts someone?""It wasn't my fault; she started it," Vesper began, wiping snot from her nose, pressing in closer to her aunt.

"Quiet, child," said Magda in a low voice before turning her attention to the small crowd, giving them a hard look. "That pact has kept the peace for hundreds of years, has kept us safe from Rome. So don't question the good fortune that you wake every morning as a free citizen of the empire and not a slave! Just be grateful for the sacrifices my family has made for you, for all of you!"

Gara opened her mouth to speak, but her aunt silenced her with a raised hand, putting her back to all of them. "Come, Vesper," began her aunt, wrapping an arm over her shoulders and pulling her along. "Today I must accept that you are no longer a child and that my burden has grown heavier sooner than expected."

They took a single step, and Vesper's heart skipped a beat like she'd been plunged into ice cold water. She blinked and found herself at the base of the great tree, dazed and confused, surprised to find her skin smooth and dry. Her aunt took a seat in front of her on a large root, her shoulders slumping as she let out a weary sigh. Vesper had more questions than she had words for, but something in the way her aunt looked up at the great tree made her hold her tongue.

It was strange; her aunt had always looked young and full of life. Her nut-brown skin had always been smooth and clear, without a wrinkle or even a blemish. She was ever ready with a smile on her full lips, but not now. She looked worn out, with her laugh lines deeper, and Vesper swore she saw wrinkles forming in the corners of her dark eyes. When at last she spoke, it was with a voice that was hoarse and frail. "You must control your anger, child. It is a dangerous thing for people like us, for the chosen."

Vesper folded her legs under her and sat down on the soft earth, crossed-legged, cocking her head. "I still don't even know what happened: one minute Aurelia was—"

"Forget about that foolish girl and her thick-headed mother," said Magda with a snort. "It is important to listen to what I tell you today."

"What did you mean 'people like us'?" asked Vesper, finally hearing her aunt's words.

"We may look the same, but you, me, along with some others in the village... we are different."

Vesper bit the inside of her cheek thinking of all the times her aunt appeared out of nowhere, of how they were suddenly at the base of the tree when only moments ago they were in the middle of the village. "Are you going to show me how you do that, be in a place one moment and then in another without moving? You said that you would show me."

Magda smiled at her, and some of her vigor somewhat returned. "You always want to run before you can walk, don't you, child. No, today I will give you a gift that will keep you safe... keep everyone safe." Vesper gasped when her aunt raised a finger and it began to glow with a soft white light. "I will need you to remove your tunic... please."

Unable to pull her gaze away, Vesper did as she was told, shivering despite the heat when she tossed aside the linen top she wore. "I'm scared."

"Don't be. You are about to begin a grand journey," said her aunt, moving in closer and touching her exposed chest with her glowing finger, continuing in a voice which was little more than a whisper. "This place, this tree, is special. Never forget that."

She winced, a gasp escaping her lips. "It hurts," she said, trying to squirm away from the burning pain that shot through her chest, only to find herself held in place by a force she couldn't see.

Her aunt continued, ignoring her struggle, her pain. "Here in this grove, under this tree, the veil between worlds is thin, things that are normally not possible are possible."

"Like making your finger glow like that," said Vesper, sucking in deep quick breaths and steeling herself against the pain. Part of her was terrified of what was happening, but her curiosity got the better of her, and she couldn't tear her gaze away from what Magda was doing. Her aunt had never hurt her, had never even raised a finger to punish her. Most of the parents in their village had no qualms about using a strap, or a switch, on sensitive bottoms, but Magda had always turned up her nose whenever she had witnessed such things in Vesper's presence, calling the whole idea of hurting a child barbaric.

"Yes, and much more." Vesper's brows came together while she watched her aunt trace a pattern the color of alabaster that contrasted brightly against her brown skin. At first it looked like gibberish, a child's scribble, but the longer she watched it began to take shape into something familiar. "It's a baobab, our village tree!"

Her aunt nodded, beads of sweat forming on her forehead while she worked. "The tree was here long before our people lived here, long before anyone, and hopefully will be here long after we are gone."

Vesper opened her mouth to speak only to be silenced when she realized her aunt was changing before her eyes. Her skin, normally dark and smooth, was covered in concentric patterns similar in color to the tree she was drawing on Vesper's chest, "What's happening to you, to your eyes," she asked when the irises in Magda's brown eyes took on a bright green hue that seemed to drink in the light.

"What you see on my skin is the story of my life, child, every moment of my journey through this world. What you see in my eyes is the energy of this sacred place here. I am a conduit for nature's energy."

"Nature's energy? I don't understand: it's just a tree, a plant."

"Nature's energy is the fire that drives all creation. It springs from all things; it surrounds us. You can feel it in the tree at your back, or the rock on which you sit, even the dirt under your feet. It is the spark of life, and the path to our power."

Vesper stared wide-eyed at her aunt, digging her toes into the mossy earth, it's cool dampness sending gooseflesh up and down her arms, an odd contrast to the burning on her skin. "The dirt is icky and cold. It's just dirt."

Her aunt's face lost some of its intensity and stretched to a warm smile, her green eyes bright against her weathered, sun-kissed skin. "Even the tiniest speck of dirt is full of life, full of power," she said, digging her free hand into the sod and showing her a handful of dark earth, "and through our gifts, we are conduits, vessels that can transform this crude matter into something wonderful."

Vesper gasped in awe when the soil in her aunt's hand began to glow like sunlight shimmering through water, floating above her open palm. "It's so pretty," she said, cocking her head, not daring to blink."

The dirt in Magda's hand swirled and sparkled, growing and expanding until circling them both like a dust devil. "The Romans, in their childish understanding of the world, tell that the gods are responsible for such things," continued her aunt. The dust devil concentrated into a small ball of flame that floated above them, glowing brightly. "They say that the gods drag the sun across the sky each day, that the gods control the seas and the harvest. Even life and death, they judge you for your deeds after you have passed and cradle you in their warm embrace if you have lived a good life by their standards."

"The gods don't exist?"

"I don't know, child. I can't say for certain. But I know of the Loa, of the spirits of our ancestors that can do great things," said her aunt, taking the ball of flame and closing her hand around it to make a fist, "But they are nothing like the Romans' say. I know there is more: I have seen it with my own eyes, read stories of Loa that can do as the gods do, make flames so bright that the sun looks dim by comparison, or part the sea so that an entire civilization can cross it."

"Can you do such things?" said Vesper, her eyes growing wider with every word that fell from her aunt's lips.

Magda shook her head, the weariness returning to her eyes. "No, the world has changed too much. What was possible long ago, is no longer possible today."

"Why not?"

"Some say that we've simply lost the wisdom to know such things," said her aunt with a shrug. "Or that our blood has thinned with time, and we lack the connection to draw deeply enough on the power that exists all around us. But I believe that we have become closed off to the wonders of the world. The Romans, in their desire to define reality, have limited it. As a people, they lack imagination, and their boring, mundane view of reality has locked the world into their version, and no other version can come forth... but I have explained enough for now. Quiet yourself so I can finish my work."

Vesper nodded, her thoughts racing while she watched her aunt draw the image of the tree on her flat chest, fascinated by how she brought even the most minute detail to life, of how every branch and bit of rough bark looked real, so much so that she could almost hear the rustle of the wind passing through its leaves, smell the sweet scent of its fruit.

The glow around her aunt's finger faded and just as quickly as it had begun, it was over with only a slight lingering pain on her skin. Magda stood and stepped back, admiring her work. "Not my best work but it will do in a hurry," she said, dry-washing her hands and nodding with approval.

Vesper looked down at the fine work that began just below her shoulder blade and ended just above her womanhood, a small smile creeping to her face as an idea sprung to mind. "So does that mean I can do the things you do, jump from place to place? Or make glowing balls of flame appear above my palm?"

Magda gave her an incredulous look as she laughed so hard Vesper was sure they heard her at the heart of the village. "No, girl! These things will take years to learn, and a lifetime to perfect. In this instance you truly must learn to walk before you run."

"Then why in the name of the gods did you put this silly thing on my chest?" she shot back, stung by the older woman's mockery.

"The heart rune is the beginning of understanding. I put it there so that I can teach you, to protect you, so you don't have to live with the guilt of murdering some poor fool who angers you because you cannot control yourself."

"I don't understand," she said, tracing a finger over the fresh lines burned into her chest, lost in the infinite pattern of the tree.

"You don't have to understand, child. You simply must trust me," said Magda, clapping her hands together. "Tomorrow I will begin to teach you, but for one last day, you will see the world like everyone else does, and be grateful for your time spent in ignorance. We will go home, have a fine meal, and spend the evening gazing at the stars one last time."

THREE

AȘẸ

The very next morning, as promised, her training began. Vesper wasn't sure what to expect, but when she was drifting off to sleep the night before, she imagined her aunt throwing off the veil of secrecy and showing her the mysteries of the world, perhaps making little mischievous dust devils and sending them all over the village, or at the very least throwing flickering balls of flame in the air, but they did none of that.

"Today you will join me in the garden," Began her aunt, her round face stretching into a joyful smile, "You will—"

"The garden!" said Vesper, her brows coming together in confusion. "But I already know all that; you taught me about herbs when I was little."

"You are still little to me, child," she said, "and as I recall you spent most of your time in my garden eating blackberries and chewing on my mint leaves."

"But—"

"Vesper, please. You have a great deal to learn, and I have very little time to teach you before you become dangerous. The more time that passes without you being in control, the more difficult this will become, so for once in your life, just do as you're told, for everyone's sake." Something in the way her aunt spoke sent shivers through her body, goosebumps running up and down her forearms. Blowing out her cheeks, she nodded, following her aunt into the maze of low trees and exotic shrubs that surrounded their home.

When she was younger and her aunt had begun to teach her about plants and herbs, the garden had been a magical place of discovery, filled with vibrant flowers of every color and every shade she could imagine, and more. She could spend hours drinking in the heady aromas of purple ox-eyed daisies or golden treasure flowers, and when she could get away with it and not hurt herself, break off pieces of tall aloe, rubbing the cool gel on her skin and relishing in its softness afterward. Her absolute favorite was the small copse of thin trees that they used to make cinnamon.

She had gotten into a great deal of trouble one year for harvesting the bark without permission, but the wonderful spice had been so savory that it had been worth it. Magda had somehow managed to cultivate plants from all over the empire, sectioning them off in a maze that was highly efficient, allowing different types of plants and trees to thrive despite the dry climate and high heat of their province. She would use the taller plants to shade the smaller ones, plant some in dry clay, and others in deep dark loam that was strangely moist all the time.

"Pay attention, child," said her aunt, holding a common white lily up to the sun. "There is power in all living things, even a simple thing like a flower petal."

Not wanting to look foolish, Vesper nodded, not really understanding. Her aunt continued, her voice taking on a lecturing tone. "Plants are the easiest thing to draw on, with the least amount of risk to yourself."

"Risk?"

"Yes, risk. There is a physical price that must be paid. When you attempt to exert your will over the world, you become a conduit between the object and reality, and as I told you, reality does not like to be toyed with, no matter the reason. It pushes back and can do great harm to your mind and body if you're not careful."

While her aunt droned on, explaining the uses of the plant in minute detail, Vesper drew in deep breaths, filling her nostrils with the lily's sweet scent. With the plant held up to the light of the sun she could make out the tiny veins in its delicate petals, almost trace the line where the stem met the flower fading from a pale green to soft white. Among her people it was known as an arum lily, and it was often seen as a harbinger of the changing season, first blooming at the start of spring, then again in the middle of summer, and a final time during the fall months before the winter season. Winter in the valley where she lived was very much like the other seasons, hot and dry, except for the occasional cool rains that gave them a welcome relief from the deadly heat. She had heard stories of places farther south, where it got cold and snow fell. One of the elders in the village told a tale of traveling through the mountains and finding the trails blocked by ice, frozen water. She could hardly imagine it being so cold that water would freeze, but she felt a tingle of excitement course through her at the thought of the cold against her skin, of breathing in cool mountain air—

"Vesper! Stop! Stop!"

Snapping back to reality, Vesper's pulse quickened, and her eyes shot open when she found her aunt rolling on the ground clutching her forearm. A thick block of white encasing the arm, steaming in the hot sun. "What happened?" she said, rushing to her aunt's side, only to pull away in surprise when she touched it. "It's so cold!"

Magda cursed with so much rage, her eyes drilling into the ice crawling up her arm, that Vesper recoiled in fear. "I told you that you must control your thoughts, foolish girl," said her aunt just as the ice exploded into a thousand shards, showering them both with droplets of icy water, "before someone gets hurt."

Vesper sputtered, shaking her head. "Me, no that's impossible. I don't know how to—"

"But you did," said her aunt, flexing her hand that was frozen only moments before.

"I'm so sorry, Auntie, I don't know how I could do such a thing. I was just thinking about the mountains, and snow, and—"

"Enough, child!" shouted her aunt, her body shaking with rage. "You should not be able to do such things yet. I have a mind to—"

"I didn't do anything," she shot back, turning and running for the villa. She had never seen her aunt so angry even during the cinnamon incident. Vesper had never seen ice and had no idea how she could make it appear out of thin air. It seemed impossible, yet it happened. Ignoring her aunt's calls, she ran into the house, racing across the white marble tiles of the atrium, and into her room at the back of the house, grateful the morning sun had not come around yet, so it was still pleasantly cool and dark. She sat there in the dim light with her mind racing at what had happened. Thinking back, she tried to remember what she had done, how she had felt, but there was nothing she could think of. Shifting uncomfortably, she rubbed the soreness on her chest, buttoning down her tunic to look at the great tree that was now forever on her skin. For some reason the tattoo hurt more today than it had yesterday. Its colors were more vibrant as well, its green leaves fluttering like they were about to snap off. Staring hard at it, she let out a tiny gasp. There at the foot of the tree, just below her hip, was a white lily nestled among the exposed roots.

"The things we consume for power leave their mark on us."

Vesper flinched, tearing her gaze away from the fresh image on her hip to find her aunt standing like a shadow in the doorway, her lips pressed together. She gave the older woman an accusing stare, bitter words spilling from her mouth before she could think. "So you've marked me to look like some common criminal or escaped slave?"

Her aunt moved deeper into the room, unwrapping the colorful shawl she wore to protect her shoulders from the sun, with a detached calm, then in a single motion, pulling her tunic over her head and folding it neatly onto the bed. "Look at me, child. What do you see?"

Looking at her aunt's skin, Vesper blinked in surprise. It was common for many of the women in the village around her aunt's age to show signs of aging, the symbols of motherhood which they wore with pride. Stretch marks, loose skin, and the battered breasts that came with bearing children. But her aunt had never been so blessed. Even in the room's dim light she could see the older woman's skin was unblemished. Her breasts still had the fullness of youth, and her belly was taut. But what was most remarkable was the tapestry on her skin. Magda had a towering tree on her midsection much like the one she had drawn on Vesper only yesterday, but the similarity ended there. Vesper's eyes traced thousands of images running up and down her body, from colorful flowers brighter than those they had in the garden, to ferocious beasts she couldn't even imagine existed. Her arms and legs were covered in layer after layer of concentric images that flowed from the great tree, forming a tapestry that she could not tear her eyes away from. "You have spent every day of your life with me, child. do these look like the crude markings you speak of? Am I some outcast shunned by our people? Do I look like a Roman slave marked by an angry dominus?"

"No," whispered Vesper, realizing that she had always seen them but never had they drawn her attention. They had always just... been. "You're beautiful, a work of art."

"Finally, you see sense. I was beginning to worry," said her aunt, moving to sit beside her.

"Will everything I touch mark me... like the lily?"

"No, some events will stay with you for all the days of your life, while others will fade with time."

"And those, the other markings, the ones in white," said Vesper pointing at the concentric circles that appeared to be layered beneath the other tattoos. They looked remarkably simple, but when Vesper tried following the strange patterns with her eyes she got lost in their complexity.

"They are called Aṣẹ," said her aunt, tracing a circle on her forearm with her finger. "They are tools of power. We use them to focus our thoughts, to exert our will on the world so that we may define our existence."

Vesper looked away, realizing at last that she had spent the last few minutes staring at her aunt's naked body. Without another word she buttoned up her tunic and focused her attention on the small room that was hers and only hers. She didn't have much, a small desk, a cot with linen sheets, along with few dried plants and colored rocks on shelves for decorations. The only thing that was of value was a simple necklace made of jasper that she had been told once belonged to her mother. She had never worn it, but today, on impulse, she placed the necklace around her neck, humming under her breath when she saw how well it fit her.

"You look a great deal like her," said Magda, breaking the awkward silence as she followed Vesper's lead and dressing.

"I do?"

"Yes," she said, moving in close and wrapping her arms around her. "You remind me more of her everyday, and of how much I miss her."

"I will do better. I promise," she said, returning the hug.

"Now come, child, the day is still young, and I have more to show you in the garden before it gets too hot."

"Go ahead, I just want to change into something that won't get dirty so easily if we are going to be spending the rest of the morning in the dirt," said Vesper, frowning at the white tunic and skirts she wore.

"I will be in the garden."

"I'll be there soon," she said, slipping out of her clothing. Vesper cursed when the necklace caught on her tunic. She was not used to wearing jewelry and would have to make a point of being more careful. Unraveling the necklace from her shirt, her brows drew together. One of the stones, which only moments ago was a deep green, was covered in flecks on black, making the whole thing look almost sickly.

Plopping down on the bed she fingered the odd discoloration, gasping when the dark spots crept from stone to stone.

With a start she felt a jolt and jumped up from her small cot, throwing the vile thing to the floor. "I must be losing my mind," she whispered to herself, hurrying to pull on the dull gray dress she used for gardening. That's when she saw it nestled between the leaves on the lowest branches of the tree on her chest. Somehow the necklace was there: it had marked her, and she had no clue how. Panicking, she moved quickly, covering it as best she could, praying her aunt would never see it so that she would never have to explain.

FOUR

THE WEAVE

They spent the rest of the day in the garden, breaking only for a short lunch of bread, olives, and a bit of soft cheese, which she hardly touched. Vesper was too excited and had no appetite, but her aunt forced her to eat.

"What we are doing is difficult on your body. If you do not eat, you are likely to fall flat on your face from exhaustion by the time you finally find some measure of control."

"I still don't understand how I was able to do it this morning without trying, and now I can't do anything," said Vesper, tearing at a piece of bread in annoyance.

They sat facing one another beneath the shade of a baobab tree that had been here long before there was a village, and would probably be here after they were long gone. The baobab was strange looking, to say the least, with a trunk that was wider than ten men standing with their arms linked together. It was told in stories that before people were able to build houses, entire families would settle in the still living trunk of these majestic trees. It was even said among the Romans that the wood was so strong that Jupiter had trapped a titan in one.

"If you are finished murdering that piece of bread, we can continue," said her aunt, dusting a few loose crumbs from her skirts before turning her attention back to Vesper. "You must concentrate; put everything from your mind, and focus on the lily, its color, its contours, its delicate petals. Drink in its smell; let it become a part of you. Once you do that, you will begin to see the fine threads of power that hold it together, bind it to reality."

Pushing away what was left of her half-eaten meal, Vesper drew in a few deep breaths to calm herself, staring hard at the tiny flower. She did as she was told, emptying her mind and not letting it wander. They sat in silence, losing all track of time until her bottom was numb from sitting, but the longer she stared, the more ridiculous she felt. "This is stupid! You can't possibly do this every time you want to whisk yourself away or do some other fantastic thing!" she blurted out, throwing her hands up. "It would be faster to just walk."

"As you learn, it will come faster, so much so that you won't think about it, like breathing."

"It didn't feel like this last time. I didn't have to concentrate. I just did it."

"That was an accident, a freak occurrence that almost never happens."

"But when I threw Aurelia, it was the same thing," she said, thinking back to the awful moment when she had hurled her friend away in a bout of anger. "I mean, every time I've—"

"Enough!" said her aunt, pressing her lips together. "This is the way; there is no other. Now stop trying to anger me and do as you are told. We must finish this before the sun goes down or we will have to start this all over again tomorrow."

"Why?"

"From the moment you first touch your power, you open yourself to dangers you cannot imagine, and it is taking all my strength to keep you safe. There are also things that I can only teach you when the stars are in the sky, things you must learn before too much time passes. Do you understand?"

"Not really."

"Well then, if you do not understand, you just have to take my word for it and do as I say without question. Now, concentrate!" she said in a tone that meant the conversation was over.

Letting out a deep breath, Vesper swallowed her anger, twisting her lips into a polite smile before continuing. "I will do my best." Bowing her head, she closed her eyes and ignored the world, blocking out the sound of insects buzzing in the garden, pushing away the ever-present chirps of birds up in the baobab's towering branches, focusing only on her breathing. She spent the rest of the afternoon feeling like she was beating her head against a wall. No matter how calm she was or how much she managed to block out her emotions, she couldn't see the threads of power holding the flower together: it just looked like a flower wilting in the afternoon heat.

"What do I do if I get this right," said Vesper, wiping beads of sweat from her brow. "What do I do with the lily's energy?"

"Nothing," said her aunt, turning her lips down. "It is a test of perspective so that you may change the way you see the world."

Nodding, she tried again, but the deeper she delved, the harder she focused, the more she was sure that her aunt was wrong; every fiber of her soul told her this was not the way. Ignoring Magda's voice, she went back to both moments, trying to remember the feeling, the emotion. She had been hurt and angry at Aurelia's words and wanted nothing more than to make her stop talking, she had been that angry. Then this morning she had been thinking about how she had never seen ice, how cold it must be, and how nice it would be in dealing with the heat. Vesper blinked, and suddenly the flower in her aunt's hand pulsed like a beating heart, a soft glow appearing around it, flickering like a candle in the wind. On impulse she reached out, cupping the soft glow in her hands and drawing it in close to her chest like a precious gift.

"Vesper, stop!" screamed a muffled voice, sounding as if it was coming from far away.

She cocked her head, unable to tear her eyes away from the glow, relishing in its warmth, feeling like she was floating in a bubble of pure joy.

"You must listen to me. Come back, child!"

Filaments of bright light shot out from the ball of energy cradled in her hands, and a smile creeped across Vesper's face as she followed the threads, each one casting out to touch a tree or a bush close by. She finally gazed at the voice screeching at her, only to find her aunt looming over her with a wide-eyed look of terror on her face. "It's so beautiful," she said, her breath catching in her throat. Looking around, her jaw fell open. The entire garden was covered in a vast tapestry of light. Hundreds, thousands of glowing threads woven together, all connected as far as she could see. Not knowing how, she pulled at the single thread that connected the tiny lily to the others, and she nearly fell from the surge of adrenaline that pulsed through her body. In front of her, Magda reached out to touch her, and Vesper had the urge to run, to get away, to be somewhere safe. And then, at the speed of thought, she was. In a rush of color, the garden, her aunt. All of it vanished and she found herself high in the great tree, a thick filament of light vibrating in front of her eyes. She smiled with glee when she understood that this was her aunt's trick, how she traveled from place to place, riding the connection between the plants in the garden and the great tree.

Howling with joy, Vesper grasped the filaments, jumping from branch to branch without moving, from the exposed roots to the highest point she could never reach by climbing, riding the paths of light that connected them all, hardly able to contain her laughter. From the top of the great tree she saw more connections spreading out beyond their village, an infinite number of glowing paths that vanished over the horizon.

Curious, she touched one, relishing in the rush of movement that sent tingles down her spine. Her village, the only place in the world she had ever known, vanished, and she found herself on a high cliff beside a small pool of blue-green water in a garden that overlooked a sea of golden sand as far as the eye could see, the sun beating down on her like a hammer. She touched another and she jumped again. This time she was lost in a sea of cool green with soft brown earth under her feet, a canopy of trees and plants towering overhead and blocking out the sun. All around her, birds she had never seen before sang and chirped, and she flinched when in the distance she heard the haunting screech of some strange beast she couldn't identify. She reached out to touch another string when a shadow fell over her.

"That is enough, child," said her aunt, appearing in front of her, blocking her path just before she could jump. "Time to stop this madness!"

Vesper opened her mouth to protest when the world shifted again and she found herself back in the garden where they had started. Magda made a swift cutting motion and the bright tapestry of the weave vanished, leaving Vesper staring at a world that was dull and faded by comparison. With a gasp she fell to the ground face-first, drenched in sweat, and her limbs trembling like she had just run the entire length of the village. She lay there clutching at a pain in her side, sucking in deep shuddering breaths, trying to calm her pounding heart. Rolling onto her back she found her aunt standing over staring, her face haggard, sweat dripping off of her temples. "I'm sorry, Auntie," she said, trying to sit up and thinking the better of it after the world started spinning.

"Sorry? Is that all you have to say! Have you lost your mind?" she said, crossing her arms under her breasts. "You could have died, or worse, killed someone with the amount of power you were drawing on."

"I just did what you asked," she said, trying not to smile when she remembered the rush of adrenaline coursing through her blood, the wonder of traveling along the threads of the tapestry.

"Fool girl! I asked you to focus on a single lily to see the energy nesting in its fragile petals, but no! As always, you must run before you walk. Look at what you have done!"

"What did I—" she began, only to have her voice catch in her throat. The garden had gone from a pallet of vibrant color to a uniform shade of dull gray, or worse, was simply gone, leaving a pile of dark ash that swirled like little dust devils in the blowing wind. "How?"

Her aunt let out a deep sigh. "When I told you about energy, did you not listen? The weave connects all life, but energy is not finite. Just as if you had walked across the village takes strength from you, the cost to flitter from place to place must be paid, and you, my child, destroyed my garden to pay for your amusements."

"I'm sor—"

"Sorry!" snapped her aunt. "Yes, I'm sure you are. But it doesn't change what you've done nor does it change what we need to do. Go to the house, get some rest. You will need it for tonight."

Vesper opened her mouth to apologize once more but thought better of it when she saw the fury in her aunt's eyes. Thinking it would be better to apologize later, she rose to her feet on legs that shook like a newborn foal, and without another word she stumbled her way into the house, using the walls to hold herself up until she made it to her room. She fell into the narrow bed and sighed, exhausted yet strangely satisfied. She had been right. She found her own way to do things even if her aunt had told her they were wrong. Her eyelids were heavy, and sleep came easily as she drifted off with a wide smile on her face, dreaming of a warm web of light covering her, connecting her to everyone and everything, content at what she had done, and excited for the future.

FIVE

THE NIGHT SKY

The girl's eyes looked strangely familiar, and she could swear they had met, but Vesper couldn't be sure where. They sat cross-legged facing one another, with a small circle drawn in the dirt between them. In the circle were a dozen colored stones, smooth and almost perfectly round.

"Are you going to look at the stones all day or are going to play?" said the strange girl, fingering a jade necklace around her neck while bouncing a large red stone in her palm.

Vesper looked up from the stones, blinking in confusion, noticing that she had a similar blue stone in her hand. The pair of them sat in the corner of a red and green striped tent packed with all sorts of dried goods, spices, herbs, and pungent-smelling teas that made her wrinkle her nose. Just a few feet away at the entrance, a heavyset woman in colorful robes of cobalt and amber haggled with a bitter-looking man in a dirty turban, all while crowds of brightly dressed men and women shuffled by.

"It's gonna be a really long game if you keep this up: just play already!"

"I don't know how to play," said Vesper, at last finding her voice. The girl in front of her was so beautiful that she couldn't help but stare. She looked young, in her early teens, but she had the figure of a grown woman, the curve of her full breasts apparent under the simple white robe she wore. She had a high forehead with full lips and deep-brown skin that was unblemished. Her black hair was plaited against her scalp and fell past her shoulders in a thick woven braid.

"That's a new one," the girl shot back, rolling her large eyes. "Are you so afraid I'll beat you again that you're playing dumb?"

"No! I swear. I really don't know how to play. Who are you? Where am I?"

"Mama, tell her she has to play. She can't spend all day fluttering around her tree."

The heavyset woman silenced the man she was talking to, with a finger and turned to give them a stern look, waving a whiplike reed at them. "Can't you children see I am with a paying customer! Lillith, stop bothering the girl. If she does not wish to play the game, let her be."

The heavyset woman returned her attention to the man with the filthy turban, and Vesper felt the tent spin, her confusion deepening. "You're Lillith?" she asked, leaning forward to balance herself against her knees. "How are you here?"

Lillith gave her a toothy smile and shrugged her shoulders. "If you want to know, you have to play the game."

"The game?" she asked, looking down to see the stones had vanished, replaced by small statues made of carved soapstone lined up against one another.

"Yes, we have to play. I'll probably win, but I'll give you a chance."

"Don't trust her, she cheats," spat the heavyset woman, glaring over her shoulder. "She'll do anything to win, that one."

"If you don't like the rules, change the game," said Lillith with a sly wink.

Vesper looked down, and the game had changed one more time. This time the circle was a square, filled with stones, some white, some black. Confused, she squeezed her eyes shut trying to remember how she had gotten here, and where was her aunt? Then in a flood of dizziness, it came back, the morning in the garden, struggling. And then finally, in the afternoon, making the connection to the lily, and then traveling to the great tree without taking a step, traveling along the connections to faraway places, so many places before finally falling exhausted in her bed. She opened her eyes to find the girl with the big eyes looking at her with a knowing smile. "It's all a dream," she said at last, nodding her head. "None of this is real."

"Life is a dream; who is to say what is real and what is not," said Lillith, fingering the jade necklace around her throat. "What matters is that we play the game to win."

Looking down, she realized the board had changed again. This time it was six evenly divided flat stones with circles drawn on them. "No, I don't think I want to play with you. It just doesn't seem fair," said Vesper, shaking her head in an attempt to force herself to wakefulness. To her relief, the tent and everything around her began to shimmer, fading like morning mist at sunrise.

The dream had almost completely faded when Lillith was suddenly at her side, gripping her shoulder. Her familiar eyes had gone from a deep brown to almost black, and her smooth unblemished skin covered in sores. "Don't worry, Vesper. Eventually, you'll play my game, but until then, I'll be watching."

Vesper awoke with a start, her heart pounding out of her chest, sweat rolling off her in waves. She sucked in huge lungfuls of air trying to calm herself while lying alone in the dark, her eyes darting in all directions as they tried to adjust. For a moment she had no idea where she was or what time it was, but the shafts of pale moonlight shining in through the high window above her bed told her it was well past sundown, and she wondered why her aunt hadn't woken her for supper. Before she could figure it out, her mind went back to what had woken her. She had never had a dream so vivid, so real. She could still smell the pungent odors of the spices in the tent, almost feel the stifling heat of the day. And where Lillith had touched her shoulder, a warmth lingered.

She jumped out of her skin when a dog barked in the distance, a small shriek escaping her lips before she could get ahold of herself. Letting out a slow breath to calm her nerves, she pushed the memory of the dream aside, instead focusing her attention on the sense of dread that was bubbling in her belly. Even in the dead of night she should hear the rustle of the leaves blowing in the wind from trees outside or the song of some distant night bird, but everything was eerily quiet, only the sound of her own breath filling her ears. Part of her wanted to crawl under the bed and hide, forget the last few days, but she thought better of it. At the very least she could find her aunt to make sure she was all right.

She sat up rubbing the grit from her eyes while trying to shake off the dull haze of sleep, and regretted it immediately. Her skin throbbed like she'd been burned by the sun, and her joints ached like someone had tried to pull her apart and failed. She vaguely remembered racing into her room after her aunt had scolded her. She had been fine, maybe a little tired but that was all. She had fallen into bed with her mind spinning with a mix of excitement and fear at touching the weave for the first time, of traveling along the infinite roads that all connected back to the tree of life, seeing the world as it really was.

A sharp curse from somewhere outside pulled her attention back to the moment, and Vesper's curiosity got the best of her. Wincing through the pain, she stood on shaky legs to go find out what was going on, thinking it would be better if she left behind the terra-cotta lamp she normally used at this time of night, not wanting its flickering light to draw attention to her.

.

Her aunt had been adamant that she begin her training today and had told her how important tonight would be, explaining to her over and over again that it was a dangerous time if she couldn't learn to control her gifts.

Making her way across the cool tile, with as much stealth as she could muster, Vesper strained to hear something, anything that would give her a clue as to where her aunt was and what was going on, but there was only silence. When she reached the front of the house, her breath caught in her throat when she heard raised voices arguing in tones bristling with anger.

"I can't do this anymore: the girl is willful, stubborn. Her mother was the same way," said her aunt.

"You chose the duty of preparing her, to see that her power was leashed!" said a voice that echoed like whispers on the wind. "I've spoken with the other guardians. Their children are all under control."

The hair on Vesper's arms raised as a chill ran through her. What were they going on about; what was she preparing her for, and what other children were they talking about? "She is not like the others," said her aunt with a tremble in her voice. "What she can—"

"Excuses will not protect our people, Magda. This crisis grows with each passing day. The children must be ready to take up the mantle. Marcus Aurelius, the emperor is not well and—"

"Don't you think I know that!" snapped her aunt. "And if you don't believe me, come see her for yourself. Or even better, I will have her come to you. She was halfway to Rome when I caught up with her earlier today and completely destroyed my garden in the process."

"Impossible! It takes years to—"

"She did! I swear it. She drained every last drop of Aṣẹ from my garden and would have killed herself if I didn't manage to stop her, and even then it was a close thing."

The other voice fell silent, and Vesper bit her lip, bowing her head in worry. Her aunt's words were cold, dismissive, without a trace of affection. It was like she was discussing a herb or plant in her garden or some weed she could easily discard.

"I'm sorry I doubted you," said the voice at last, speaking slower, almost pensive. "Where is the girl now?"

Her aunt let out a deep sigh, and when she spoke, there was a tremor in her voice. "I have cast her into torpor. Hopefully they won't reach her if she is in a dreamless sleep. I will have to restart her training tomorrow."

"You're playing a dangerous game, Magda, if you've waited too long—"

"I have not!" said Magda in a stern tone that brooked no argument. "This came on much faster than anticipated, but if I must, I will take the necessary steps to protect us all."

"You would do such a thing to your own blood?"

"As you said... I swore an oath to protect this world," said Magda. "I will do what I must."

"Then I pray that you are right. And if you're not, it is my hope that the other children will be enough."

Vesper clutched her midsection, her stomach turning like someone had kicked her in the gut. They were supposed to be family, but with every word her aunt spoke to the strange voice, she realized her entire life was all a lie. The woman who was raising her, who she thought loved her, didn't care. She only took care of her because of some oath, out of a sense of duty, worse if Vesper understood what was being discussed, she would be cast aside if her aunt decided it was necessary. Squeezing her eyes shut, she pushed back tears. It would do her no good to show weakness now, like she was some small child that needed to be coddled. She would show her aunt how defiant she could be. Ignoring the pain in her limbs and the ache on her skin, she stood up straight despite her shaking legs. Raising her chin high, she stepped out to confront her aunt.

She walked out of the house with hateful words on the tip of her tongue, ready to scream, to fight. Then before she could say anything, the words caught in her throat, her mouth going dry the moment she looked up dumbfounded at the night sky.

"It is wondrous, is it not?" said her aunt, breaking the silence with quiet words and a knowing smile, looking not the least bit surprised to find her in the doorway. "This is what you were meant to see, to hear, and hopefully, understand. It is time you learned your place in this world, for better or worse."

SIX

THE OSE

Vesper's mouth fell open as she gazed at the heavens with wonder, her anger, a blazing torrent only moments before, forgotten like it never was. "How? W-what did you do to me? H-have I lost my mind?" she stammered, sure that what she was seeing was some sort of trick. Finally, with a supreme effort, she tore her gaze away and gave her aunt a questioning look.

"I have done nothing. Your eyes are now open, child," said her aunt, spreading her arms wide. "The threads of power you touched earlier today were just the beginning: now the curtain of reality has been pulled back for you so that you may see the truth."

"This can't be real?" whispered Vesper with a shudder, full of doubt, but somehow knowing in her heart that what she was seeing was real. "Can it? I mean... what is it?"

"This is the story of humanity from the very first moment that our minds touched the world to this very instant. Every life, every breath. All of the love and hate, each victory or defeat. Our story, told among the stars."

Her aunt was right. The stars were still there, glowing brightly against the curtain of night, but they were covered and connected by a shimmer of subtly flashing images that were a confusing jumble at first, but the more she looked, the clearer they became, and understanding blossomed in her mind. The threads she had seen in the afternoon were there, more than she could possibly ever count in a single lifetime, all of them connected by the stars, forming a vast weave of pictures, each so tiny that they were almost impossible to see, unless... she focused. "That's me!" she said, blinking in surprise, and pointing with excitement.

Her aunt's face split into a wide grin, a look of pride filling her eyes. "Yes. Our own threads are often easiest to follow, along with those that are the closest to us. Family, friends, those we love, and who love us. They pull at us the most, forming bonds that are forever etched into eternity."

Vesper nodded absently, followed the glowing threads with a childish grin plastered on her face, easily identifying her aunt by the thick gray braids framing her round face, and on the other side of her own image, farther away, was her father in his robes of state, looking almost Roman despite this dark skin. She could make out friends she played with from the village, and if she went further out from her small family, she found people she had met only briefly. "Where is my mother?" she blurted out, scanning the threads spreading out from her image.

There was a long pause, and Vesper wondered if her aunt had heard her. With a start she looked over to see the older woman's face was a mask of pain, and her eyes were bright with unshed tears. "I'm sorry, child, your mother chose to no longer be part of this world; she is lost to us."

"I don't understand," she began, only to be silenced by her aunt, shaking her head.

"I am sorry. It's.. it's... too painful to explain. Ask me again one day, when times are not so desperate."

"What do you mean 'desperate'?" asked Vesper, hungry to know what was going on. "And who were you talking to, and why would you say—"

Her aunt sighed, pressing her lips together. Without a word she opened her arms and motioned for her to come closer, pulling her into a warm hug. Vesper hesitated at first, resisting with a bit of childish anger, but after a moment she collapsed into her embrace, grateful for the affection. "I'm sorry, child. I wish I could make this easier for you. I wish you could have a normal childhood, like Lillith and I did, but that will be impossible now," she said, rubbing small circles on her back. "I must teach you quickly, before it's too late."

"Too late for what?"

"I want you to look at the sky and tell me what you see, not just the stars and the images, but all of it, taken as a whole."

Vesper snorted, pushing away from her aunt and turning her eyes once more to the spectacle in the sky. The images were like a mirage, shimmering in the distance, and their beauty, the fine detail became more pronounced the longer she looked, the more it took her breath away. She was sure she could spend a lifetime and more studying it, learning from it; part of her wondered if some, like her aunt, did just that. Without knowing how, she followed a thread that led to her father, and then she followed one to her father's father, and on, and on. Each strand weaving from one life to another, family lines stretching back through an infinite number of souls. "It's like reading a story, each thread telling a tale of how a person lived, who they touched, even how they died. I can see the love, the pain, all of it."

"Very good, child, and what else?"

"I'm not sure," she said, narrowing her eyes as a thought came to her. "Is this why we spend our evenings looking at the stars, so you can watch this?"

"Yes. Don't let yourself be distracted by random thoughts, focus."

She did as she was was told, pushing all the questions swirling around in her head. Trying to take it all in, she felt lost. There was too much, too many lives, too many stories. It all seemed like a jumbled mess, and she had no idea where to start. One moment she was looking far into the past at the lives of slaves in faraway Egypt, forced to build towering pyramids under vicious lashes of the whip, dying forgotten after short and brutal lives. Then just as quickly she was following the thread of a handsome Roman boy on a hill, overlooking a vineyard of bright green grapes growing from black earth, so beautiful that she could almost taste wine on her tongue. Vesper moved on to watching a dimple-faced woman wrap her hair while getting ready for sleep, singing softly under her breath to a girl who had the same eyes as she did. "I see Aurelia! And her mother!" said Vesper excitedly, understanding dawning. "It's not just the past! I see what's happening now."

"Yes, sometimes if you are close or have something that belongs to the person."

"So I can spy on people in the village?" She giggled, her eyebrows raising with thoughts of mischief.

"This is not a thing to be abused. You cannot behave like a child," said her aunt, looking serious for a moment before breaking into a small laugh. "But it never hurts to peek."

"Exactly. It's just a little fun. Besides, who will know?"

Her aunt went on trying to be serious, but the twinkle in her eye made it clear that she peeked often enough. Pushing her aunt's words to a droning buzz, Vesper focused on the threads extending out from her own tiny image. She found her father again, off to the side, wondering why he was so far from her, why there was so much space between them. Part of her was drawn to that open space, and the longer she stared, the larger it grew and she felt like she was being drawn in, pulled into some dark void that had no end. In a heartbeat, all the images around her had vanished and there was only the void. Then she saw it and her heart almost stopped. "It's not a space; there used to be an image there; she's missing, gone," she said, going in closer now, gooseflesh tingling up and down her arms despite the stifling nighttime heat.

"Yes, child, torn from existence, like she never existed."

Not knowing how, Vesper went deeper, coming so close that she could see the threads in that area were ragged and torn, like fragile bits of cloth worn by time... and beyond, there was only darkness, and something else, a sound of some kind. A dissonant whisper that echoed back and forth so softly that she couldn't understand the words or even find the direction of its source. Narrowing her eye, Vesper looked around, pulling her vision back to see better, and for the first time noticing the void wasn't unique and a multitude of ragged holes were scattered across the tapestry.

"Come back, girl! You go too far," said her aunt, her voice small and distant.

Vesper tried to pull away, but her limbs refused to listen to her, like she was in a dream and couldn't wake, couldn't move... and deep down, part of her wanted to hear more, to decipher the haunting words spilling from the void. "I can almost understand. I can hear my name. It knows me," she said in an excited voice, her ears straining to make out the alien tongue while she dove in deeper, an icy cold washing over her useless limbs.

Vesper gasped in pain when a brilliant flare of light exploded in her face, blinding her, and knocking her onto her bottom.

"As always, you run before you can walk," she heard her aunt say as she blinked away afterimages dancing in her vision.

"Why did you do that? I was so close. I could almost understand what it was saying," she said, finding herself sitting in the dirt, a prickling, painful sensation like needles piercing her skin, running up and down her body.

Her aunt plopped down beside her and let out a deep sigh. Vesper was sure she was about to be berated once more for being headstrong, for doing what came naturally to her, but instead her aunt ran the pads of her fingers over Vesper's skin, like she was painting a picture, and the ice cold vanished like it never had been, and control returned to her limbs, and her aunt smiled at her when she began wiggling her hands and toes. "I swear if I don't stop you, you'll be the death of me, girl,"

"I'm sorry, Auntie, I don't know—"

"Don't worry, child. Even if I wanted to, it seems that I cannot stop you. You grow in skill faster than anyone I have ever seen," she said. "But still, you must be careful. The weave is not what it once was. It's dangerous, and we can't afford to lose you."

"It looks like it's been damaged, parts of it burnt away," said Vesper, thinking about what she had seen, what she had felt. "And who exactly is we?"

"Come, let's get off the ground and I will do my best to explain," said her aunt, motioning to the bench where they spent most of their evenings gazing at the stars.

Vesper sat down with a sigh, embracing the feeling of doing something routine, doing something they did every night as if nothing had changed, but then she looked up and her pulse quickened once again, a cold fear sitting heavy in the pit of her stomach. "My ears are open?"

Her aunt looked down at her hands, a fierce look coming to her face as she began, "Once, long ago in a different age, before the Romans ruled these lands, before men learned to write and record history, when even the stars in the sky were different, our people, the Ose, ruled over a vast empire, so great that the entire continent bowed down to us. We were admired... and feared. We grew great baobab trees, trees grander than these tiny things you see now, trees that lived for thousands of years. Reality bent to our will because our control over the weave was absolute."

Her aunt pointed at a part of the sky, and Vesper saw the dawn of history and the bones of an empire that stretched across the known world, an empire lost to the sands of time. "But as our empire grew, so did our arrogance, and with time, Olodumare, the almighty creator punished us, limiting our power over his creation. The weave, once easily guided, now fought back against us like a ship in a violent storm—the harder we fought to change its course, the more it unraveled in our hands—and after a time, all of reality threatened to come apart."

"Like the holes in the pattern now," said Vesper, eyeing the rotting holes in the fabric of reality that she was just now starting to see with some clarity.

"Yes," said her aunt, nodding. "But far worse. We lost a millennia of history, with parts of the world simply vanishing as if they never existed. But before the world would be lost to us, it was decided that we would limit the use of our power, stop trying to replace God by bending reality to our will. Where once everyone could tap into the weave, we limited power to only a chosen few, and even then they were taught to be subtle, to not rock the boat as it were. We had learned that small changes did less damage, were easier, and that grand displays were no longer tolerated, or in some cases no longer even possible."

"And did the pattern heal, repair itself?" asked Vesper, her curiosity peaked.

"In some ways yes, but there were parts of reality that had already been completely wiped from existence, continents that ceased to exist never returned. With time, because we lacked the power we once had, our empire shrank, and then vanished. The ancient baobab trees, once a symbol of our power, withered and died without our will to keep them going. They became a shadow of their former selves, and now all that remains of us, of the Ose, are a few scattered villages, struggling to scrape together enough grain to sell to the Romans for protection against enemies with a long memory of the indignities we caused them under our heels, enemies who grow stronger with each day."

Vesper crossed her arms and leaned back, her mind reeling. Parts of it seemed impossible to believe, to think that so much power existed, the power to change the entire world. It was impossible... or was it? She herself had done the impossible only this morning, traveling miles in the blink of an eye, drawing on power she could hardly understand, much less control. Sucking in a deep breath filled with the odor of night-blooming jasmine, she eyed the thread that led to her lonely image floating above, twinkling in the night sky. "And what of me? what do you have planned for my future?"

"It has been a long day," said her aunt, looking away. "Perhaps it would be best if we—"

"No!" said Vesper louder than she had intended but still not backing down. "The person you were talking to—they said there were others, that we needed to take up the mantle?"

Her aunt stood up, stretching like a cat before motioning for her to take her hand. "Very well, we have already begun this journey: we might as well finish it. Come with me and I will show you."

Vesper hesitated for a moment before taking her aunt's hand, surprised that she had given in so easily. The day had been full of so many wonders that it had made her head spin, and she couldn't imagine what else could possibly happen, but she braced herself for the worst and reached out. Even knowing what to expect, a smile came to her face as the world shifted all around her, and they bounded along the lines of power, each step taking them miles at a time, the mundane world rushing past them in a blur of dark skies and bright stars.

Just as quickly as it had begun, it was over, and Vesper found herself standing atop a dark hill overlooking a vast city, bright with flickering lights that pushed back the night, amazed at the sheer size of it. "It's beautiful," she said, her breath catching in her throat. "How do they keep it all lit?"

"A million lights from a million decadent souls," muttered her aunt under her breath, a frown coming to her face. "Welcome to Rome, my child. The beauty you see is their decadence, their defiance of the natural order. These fools are so afraid of the night that they drink the empire dry of oil to push away the dark."

"This is Palatine Hill," she said, staring in wonder. "Look, there is the temple of Saturn, and over there is the forum with all the statues, just like in the books Father gave me." From a young age Vesper had read stories of this place. She had spent hours staring at drawings of its most important landmarks. With her finger she traced the massive stone aqueducts that fed the city's dazzling array of baths and fountains, but her books could never prepare her for the stunning view that filled her eyes. This was no backward village on the edge of civilization where the day ended when the sun went down. The city stayed awake when night fell, and Vesper found herself gaping at the tall marble buildings, majestic works of art in their own right, glowing under the light of thousands of lamps. In the distance her ear caught the melody of a high-pitched harp, and she could almost hear voices raised in song as if some sort of celebration was going on. "Is it a festival of some kind that we don't celebrate, or someone's birthday?" asked Vesper.

Magda snorted, shaking her head. "More than likely, but these people need little excuse to celebrate, drinking and carousing till all hours of the night without sense. It is a vile place and we will not stay long."

Vesper flinched at the intensity in her aunt's voice, and she looked over to see hatred gleaming in her dark eyes, and something more, something she couldn't understand. She knew her aunt well. They had spent every waking moment together, and Vesper had never known her to show emotions so openly, so raw. Looking out over the gleaming city, her mind was flooded with questions, but she thought better than to ask, given her aunt's mood. "Why are we here, then?" she asked.

Her aunt didn't look at her, simply droning on in a voice that was cold and distant. "The Ose, that is what we call our people, can mean many things depending on the tongue that speaks it. Bold, daring, and even brave. These Romans speak of us in whispers only, grudgingly accepting us, but if they had a choice they would prefer that we not exist: they call us the demon people. But among our own, it means chosen."

"Chosen?"

"Yes," she said, nodding her head. "Long ago we were chosen to rule over this land, but as I told you, we grew arrogant and were punished for our sins. After, it became our duty to protect it."

"From what, drunken Romans?" said Vesper with a nervous laugh, trying to lighten her aunt's mood.

"No, child. This city is the heart of a great empire. What happens here echoes across the lives of millions of people that live under its rule: the world looks to Rome for direction... but let me ask you, can you see the weave here? Do you see the threads that connect the lives of those who live here?"

Vesper's brows came together as she looked out over the flickering lights, her mind reeling when she realized what she saw or didn't see. "No... it's like there's nothing here."

A chill washed over her when her aunt waved a hand, muttering strange words under her breath. The glowing city faded from her sight when the weave became more apparent, revealing the ragged tapestry hanging over the city, "To the untrained eye the city is a beacon of hope, but under the surface, if one looks closely, it is a festering cesspool, one that will spill over and consume everything in its path unless we remain vigilant."

Vesper stood stock still, unable to tear her eyes away. When she had seen the small tears in the pattern earlier that night, it had terrified her, the empty voids floating among the stars making her belly turn with nausea, but this, this was something worse. Entire swaths of the pattern were gone, with not a thread in sight that connected those in the city to the outside world. This place was barren, consumed by darkness. "How did this happen?" she asked, finding her voice at last.

"We don't know. Lust, greed, envy. No one can be sure, but by the time we realized what was happening, it was too late. The more this void grows, the greater the madness among the people, its corruption growing like a stain on the souls of all who live here. All we could do was try to hold it altogether. Since the time of Augustus, the Roman emperors have been wise enough to understand the danger and they have been our allies. Augustus himself founded the praetorian guard with the hope to help protect Rome from this madness, and the most powerful among the chosen stand with them in holding back the darkness that threatens to overflow and poison the rest of the world. People like your father... your mother as well."

"My mother?" said Vesper, her head whipping around to look at her aunt. "She lived here; is this why her image is gone from the pattern. The void took her?"

Magda sighed, pressing her lips together before continuing. "After a fashion, but that does not matter now: what happened to your mother is far in the past. What concerns us is the future, your future."

Vesper's brows drew together at her aunt's words, her first thought being that the older woman had lost her mind. "You want me to... to what?"

"I want you to control yourself. I want you to listen when I speak and not run off face-first into danger like some fool Roman."

"Yes but—"

"And no more talking back either... there is too much at risk."

Vesper pressed her lips together, swallowing the denial that was at the tip of her tongue, instead raising her chin and lowering her eyes in acceptance.

"Very good, child," said her aunt, looking back toward the city and pointing. "Now, as I was saying. Our long-standing agreement with the empire is that one of the chosen serves as the emperor's hand, using our power, our ability to manipulate the weave to protect the world from the dark forces that threaten to consume it. This was your mother's duty for a time and is your father's duty now."

"I thought you said my mother was a fierce protector of our people, that our enemies feared her—" she began, only to catch herself and then swallow her tongue. "Sorry, go on."

"Your mother was very powerful, and her very name made our enemies tremble in fear, but she did it from here, from Rome. She and the emperor were closer than most, and he gave her a great deal of freedom to carry out her duties as his hand, and she used that freedom to see our enemies crushed by Roman legions."

Vesper wrapped her arms around herself as she looked out over the bright city, the hair on her arms standing on end. She was still in awe of its beauty, its majesty, but now she was terrified of it. "Is that what you were talking about before.? Am I meant to serve here?"

"It is not certain: you and the other children will be tested, and the strongest will represent our people and serve as hand."

"What about my father?" asked Vesper.

"The role of hand is a difficult one, thankless in many ways. The power required to stand against Rome's vileness wears on a person, grinds them down like stone used to mill flour, and as a result, your father's health is failing. So we have taken the example of the emperor's, to begin training replacements while the current hand is still serving. Just as the emperor's son, Commodus, is being groomed to replace him, one of the children will join your father in Rome, and replace him when the time comes."

She had seen her father only a few times over the last few years, and his visits were so short that she hardly knew him. He was a stranger to her, a distant figure that she knew only from her aunt's stories. Growing up, she had been resentful that he was away so much, but with time she understood that his position meant that they lived a far better life than most of the people in their village, and she was grateful for that. Now that she knew it cost him his health, his life, she felt a strange mix of guilt and determination. The very least she could do to honor him would be to follow in the path he had laid down for her, bring honor to her people while making the world a better place. "I will meet any challenge you place in my path," she said, drawing in a deep breath, turning to face her aunt. "I will be better, stronger than anyone else. I swear."

Magda's wide smile returned, and she patted Vesper on the cheek. "Very good, child, I have never been so proud."

"So when do we begin?"

"Tomorrow, with the rising sun, the elders and myself will begin training you and the others. I promise you, it will be difficult, but you will learn such things that your head will spin with wonder," she said, extending her hand once more. "Now let us return home. We have spent too long wallowing in Roman filth."

Vesper smiled, taking her aunt's hand, giving it a squeeze full of warmth and affection. In the blink of an eye, the hilltop and the majestic city with its bright lights was gone, replaced by the simple village that she called home. Part of her wondered if she would look at it the same way after witnessing the glory of Rome with its million flickering lights and titanic column of marble. In the distance she heard a sharp cry, and for a moment she thought it was a scream. She turned to face their little hamlet, curious as to what could have made such a noise, expecting that at this time of night it would be mostly dark, with maybe a few torches or hearths burning low, but instead the night was aglow: orange flame blazing against the black sky. Sparks of red and ocher looking like a million fireflies were dancing above the flames. The screams were her people, and the village burned.

SEVEN

CULLING

Earlier in the day, in this very garden, it had taken every ounce of her focus to see the threads of power springing from a single lily cupped in her aunt's palms, to touch the energy trapped in its delicate petals. Now, seeing her home burn, Vesper didn't think. She reacted, drinking in a torrent of power from what was left of her aunt's vast collection of plants, and then in a rush, she jumped. Vanishing from the garden and riding the thread that led to the massive baobab tree at the heart of their now burning village.

In the span of a single breath, Vesper appeared at the base of the great tree, expecting to be alone among its exposed roots so that she could catch a glimpse of what was going on. To her shock she came upon a small group of men with torches trying to set the roots of the baobab on fire. They were like nothing she had ever seen, tall and heavyset, thick through the middle. Their dark skin and faces were covered in white markings, each of them having a pair of bleached horns curving down the sides of their heads, making them appear demonic. It took her a moment to realize they were animal bones of some kind, and they painted themselves with the intent to frighten, to terrorize.

"Kill her!" one of them shouted, and with a start, she realized they had seen her. Two of them men peeled off from the others, stalking toward her while brandishing wicked-looking spears capped with metal tips stained red. Vesper backed away, her hand outstretched protectively in front of her while her stomach twisted in knots. The pair of men came closer and she could almost feel the hate and anger rolling off them in waves. One of them men raised his spear to hurl it at her and the world around her seemed to slow to a crawl. Even in the dark she could see the flex of his shoulders as he pulled back, the ripple of the muscles under his skin. Vesper knew he was about to kill her without a second thought, and she realized she deserved it. She had promised her aunt only a few minutes ago, on a hill overlooking the city of Rome, that she would stop being foolish, that she would be better, and now she had done just the opposite, charging headlong into danger without a thought of what might be going on, or if she could be hurt.

She tensed as the spear left the man's hand, flying fast toward her breast. For a heartbeat she was sure that it was over, and that her short life had been for nothing. But as the weapon flew toward her it pivoted as if struck by something, its wickedly sharp tip going wide, and instead of tearing through her chest, it grazed her upper arm, leaving a bloody gash that sent waves of pain through her and knocking her to the ground. Vesper landed with a grunt on a thick root, her head bouncing off the unyielding wood. Groaning at the stinging on her arm, she fought back against a wave of nausea and dizziness that threatened to make her stomach spill its contents as she struggled to get back on her feet. Blinking away the pain in her head, Vesper turned to face her attackers and her jaw fell open. Magda, her small round-bodied aunt was standing at the center of the men with the painted faces, her normally kind face and warm smile were gone, replaced by a look of fierce determination and a snarl of anger that made Vesper terrified and proud all at once. The older woman had managed somehow to tear away a spear from one of the men, who now lay against a root, clutching at a dark stain on his belly. Vesper watched in awe as the older woman spun the weapon faster than she thought possible, using it to defend and attack all at once. In one moment she deflected a series of short vicious jabs that came in high and low, then with the men's weapons knocked wide, she slammed the butt of the weapon into one's throat before spinning it around again and using it like a sword to slash another's belly wide open, spilling the man's guts to the ground.

Magda then twisted around again, ducking to avoid a wild swing and then burying the tip of the spear into one of her attacker's calves, sending him reeling back, clutching at the pain in his leg, before reversing her grip to slam it into the groin of a warrior whose spear was raised over his head to strike her down. To Vesper's surprise the last man fighting turned on his heel, screaming in a strange tongue that she didn't understand while bounding away like a gazelle desperate to outrun a cheetah. Her aunt, undeterred, didn't waste a moment, hefting the spear over her shoulder, and then hurling the spear in a single, smooth motion. Vesper winced, her eyes flying open when the powerful throw pierced the warrior's back, sending him tumbling like a puppet whose strings had been cut, his dying body twitching in the dirt.

Vesper opened her mouth to speak, but her aunt silenced her with a look. "You stupid girl," she seethed, the thick braids framing her face shaking with rage as she stormed toward her. "You just finished promising me you would stop this foolishness, this running before you can walk. Why must you risk everything I have worked for my entire life."

"I'm sorry. I just wanted to help," said Vesper, angry at hearing her own thoughts thrown back at her. "I thought—"

"No! You did not think. You leapt off like a child, without a single notion of what was happening. You have so much potential, more than anyone I have ever met, yet you squander it like some Roman spilling wine."

"Auntie, I— Look out," Vesper caught a flicker of movement behind her aunt, almost like an afterimage of looking at the sun too long. Without thinking she hurled herself at her aunt, every muscle straining while she wrapped her arms around her waist and pushed her to one side. The weapon hissed like a serpent as it passed a hairsbreadth from her ear, the sharp taste of copper filling her mouth as she landed on top of her aunt, who squirmed and punched like a trapped animal beneath her.

"Get off me, you fool,"

Vesper did as she was told, rolling off only to find a limping warrior with a hateful glare on his face appearing above them, branding a short, curved blade, the whites of his eyes glowing in the dark. The weapon came down, and Vesper closed her eyes and raised her hands protectively over her face, bracing for the blow that would end her life. But to her surprise the blow never came, and she nervously squeezed open one eye, her brows coming together in confusion at the warrior who stood above her, somehow frozen in place, his entire body locked in the motion of bringing down his sword. She looked to find her aunt with an outstretched hand, her chest rising and falling like she had just run a race, nostrils flaring. "What happened?" said Vesper, swallowing hard.

"Take the weapon from his hand... now!" said her aunt, her body trembling.

Vesper did as she was told, quickly prying the weapon loose from the man's iron grip, looking for any hint that he would attack again. By the way his eyes darted in all directions she could tell he was still conscious... and terrified, but his body was stuck, stopped, no longer under his control. "What did you do," she whispered, her eyes flickering back and forth from her aunt to the warrior.

"Now is not the time for questions," said her aunt in a strained voice. "Take the sword and put it in his belly... quickly. Who knows how many more of them are in the village?"

Vesper let out a short gasp, swallowing hard. Looking into his eyes she could see he understood, and part of her could sense his fear. He didn't want to die, not like this, like an animal caught in a trap. "I can't," she said, her entire body shaking. "Can't we just... you know... put him to sleep or something?"

Magda's eyes drew together, and her nostrils flared, a shadow of disappointment creeping over her face. "He would end your life without a thought—he was about to," said her aunt, slowly getting to her feet, taking the blade from her hand. "His blade is stained with the blood of our people."

"I can't," she whispered, pulling back. Vesper had never hurt anyone, at least not on purpose. She was squeamish even killing chickens or goats, and the idea of killing a man, even one who would have killed her did not sit well in her heart.

"His kind, the Sandawei, they have been our enemies since before time. Look in his eyes; even now he hates us, fears us. How many men, how many women and children has he taken from us, all for a hatred long forgotten," she said, using his own blade to carve thin lines of blood across his chest.

"Don't we need to be better than our enemies," said Vesper, not sure why she was arguing for the life of a man who had just tried to kill her. "I mean, in the heat of battle, in fair combat, yes, to kill makes sense. But like this, when he is helpless?"

"Those who show mercy to their enemies, do so only to die later, on their blades," she said. "I am not so foolish, and you should not be either."

Vesper opened her mouth to protest, to say there was a better way, when the man's eyes went wide as her aunt plunged the sword into his stomach, twisting the blade with a feral grin on her face. With a growl she roughly pulled the blade out, holding the weapon up so that Vesper could see the blood on it.

"Look at it," said her aunt in a voice that brooked no argument. "It is your duty to protect your people. You must never hesitate, ever! Or one day, it will be your blood, or the blood of someone you love on the end of a blade. Understood!"

"Yes, Auntie."

"Now, come! Lives are depending on our swiftness."

Her aunt turned and raced ahead, leaving Vesper to watch the fallen Sandawei warrior bleed out on the dirt, clutching at his spilled innards. Looking into his pained face, her gaze shifted without thought, and she found herself watching the threads of his life fade away. The energy pulsing through him was like the lily from the garden, only so much more. Where the lily was a simple glowing ball of light, he was far more complicated. Now that she knew how to look and what to look for, even as his life faded, Vesper could trace a thousand lines of power splaying in all directions, connecting him to the greater world. Up above in the tapestry of night he could see those that touched him, those he loved, his wife, children, even friends. This was a man with a life who was part of the greater pattern that made up the world... and he was in pain, more pain than she could imagine. Vesper hesitated for a moment, then as if in a dream, she reached out with a trembling hand, clutching at the weak remnants of his life, just like she'd done with the lily, drawing it into her. She gasped, her head falling back as a rush of strength flooded into her limbs. She suddenly felt like she was standing under the blazing noon sun, blinded by its brightness. To her amazement she felt stronger, and was sure that she could leap to the heavens and touch the stars, or outrun a gazelle.

"Vesper!" shouted her aunt in the distance. "Stop dragging your feet in the dirt, and stay close to me."

With a start she came back to herself, choking smoke filling her nostrils, orange-and-red flames flickering in the distance. At her feet, the Sandawei warrior, with his white painted face and cruel-looking tusks affixed to the side of his head, had stopped moving, his life ended with a pitiful gasp, the brilliance that she saw only a moment ago gone. What she had taken from him, the Aṣẹ that was his life still coursing through her, was far more invigorating than the plants she had touched, far more. She felt all the stronger for it.... and deep down inside, there was a hollow ache in her belly that wasn't there before. Her aunt screamed after her and Vesper pushed the feeling aside, wondering what the hell she just did.

EIGHT

THE SANDAWEI

Vesper easily caught up to her aunt who gave her a questioning look.

"What took you so long, child?"

"Nothing," she said, hesitating, grateful that the dark hid her features and her lie. Part of her still trembled from the warm tingle still in her belly from the energy of the Sandawei, her blood still racing from the surge of Aṣẹ coursing through her. Falling in line beside her aunt, she gave the older woman a sidelong glance, wondering if she'd seen what Vesper had done even if she herself hadn't the faintest idea. It all had been wonderful, like waking from a pleasant dream or savoring the heat that lingered in her mouth after a good spicy meal. She wanted to know more but was frightened that her aunt would be angry with her if she found out, and forbid her outright from learning on her own, and that was the last thing she wanted.

"I know when you lie, girl," said her aunt, confirming Vesper's fears, "and I know what you did. It was foolish and dangerous to play with power you don't understand... but we will discuss it later. For now, keep close to me, and don't do anything else so asinine"

Vesper frowned at her aunt's back, pushing aside her worry.

Magda knew the truth of what she did to the warrior, but now was not a good time for an argument. Their home was on fire, and hopefully she would forget all this once the urgency passed. The village was laid out in a circle, with most of the homes on the outer ring, and the few shops and public spaces closer to the heart of it all. From what Vesper could see, the fire looked like it had started in the western end of town and was moving eastward, consuming everything in its path. Despite it all, her aunt thought it wise that they move slowly and keep to the shadows as they made their way toward the screams and shouts in the distance.

"Hold!" said her aunt, pulling Vesper against the wall of one of the huts they were passing. Her heart beat out of her chest as they fell back into the shadows, her ears and eyes straining to catch a hint of what her aunt had seen or heard. She flinched when a series of deep voices called out to one another in the strange Sandawei tongue, their guttural language resonating in the dark. "Follow, slowly, and not a sound," said her aunt, creeping ahead of her.

Vesper did what she was told, slowly moving with her until they caught sight of a large group of Sandawei warriors running from house to house. "What kind of monsters are these?" she said, balling her fists when she saw them roughly pulling terrified people from their homes and then using torches that stunk of dung, to set fire to the thatched roofs. The large group of men were much like the others her aunt had fought. Stout, their faces painted white, with animal tusks strapped to the sides of their heads to make them appear demonic.

"They are little more than beasts," said her aunt, her gaze never wavering. "And I will put them down like beasts."

She followed the older woman's glare, cursing under her breath when she saw that some of the Sandawei tribesmen had captured a large group of women and children, shoving them onto their knees while they bound their hands and feet with rope. "What are they doing?" she asked in harsh whisper, balling her hand into a fist when one of the white-faced warriors slammed the butt of his spear into a pregnant lady's belly.

"Preparing them," said her aunt, anger flashing in her eyes. "They will be taken to market and sold to slavers."

Vesper's brows came together and she made a face. "But they are not slaves; they are free people. How could they do such a thing."

"It is common for those taken in battle to be sold in such ways: no one questions it. The slavers are more than happy to pay, especially for women and small children."

"We can't let this happen. We must stop them," said Vesper, gritting her teeth.

"And yet you hesitated to kill the one we captured. I told you they would not show you the same mercy."

"I didn't understand. I didn't see them for what they were, but now, we must stop this. Before it's too late," said Vesper, wincing in sympathy when one of the Sandawei pulled a woman from her husband, kicking him to the dirt while he fought like a wild beast to protect her and a younger boy who bore a striking resemblance to him. Vesper felt a burning rage in her belly and was about to attack when her aunt put a restraining hand on her shoulder, shaking her head.

"No! You will do nothing; you must look, learn. I will punish these men, show them true what cruelty is. I will punish them," said her aunt, her face a mask of fury as she raised her hands.

Vesper watched in awe as her aunt tugged at the weave, gathering stray threads of it in her hand ever so gently while she muttered harsh words under her breath, her voice echoing like a whisper and a shout all at once. With her final syllable, the air stilled, unmoving like the world was holding its breath. Then it all snapped back and a powerful surge of wind blasted through the dust-covered street, whipping up a stinging wave of dirt and grit that scoured over the Sandawei warriors, tearing at exposed skin while powerful gusts threw them off-balance. Snarling in anger, her aunt raised her arms higher, pulling harder at the weave. Clumps of burning thatch and sod tore away from the burning huts, sending small balls of flame slamming into the bewildered warriors, setting their loose-fitting clothes on fire and sending most of them rolling onto the ground in a pitiful attempt to douse out the flames. To Vesper's amazement the wind and flames never touched the men and women of the village, avoiding them completely.

"Now, take this," said her aunt, shoving the spear she had taken from the other Sandawei into her hands. "I will deal with these fools, but if anyone manages to come near you, poke him with the sharp end... and Vesper, this time, do not hesitate."

"Yes Auntie," she said, baring her teeth with a snarl.

Her aunt did as before, wading into the fallen group of warriors without fear, arming herself with one of their own fallen weapons. This time a crescent-shaped, iron sword with a wickedly sharp tip. The older woman didn't hesitate, slashing and stabbing at the blinded and burning Sandawei without mercy, the heavy blade in her hand cutting through bone and flesh like a scythe.

It was over before it began, and within moments her aunt was standing over the bodies of a dozen men, bloody sword in hand while her chest heaving. Vesper narrowed her eyes, feeling like a veil had been lifted and she was seeing Magda the first time. The soft matronly woman who comforted her when she had a bad dream, or cleaned her cuts and scrapes when she fell, was gone, replaced by an otherworldly creature brimming with power, an avenger who protected her people with every ounce of her being, cutting down her enemies with vicious efficiency.

The women and children that her aunt had just saved raced to thank her, reaching out with trembling hands to touch her with wide-eyed reverence. Magda held up the bloody sword, stopping them in their tracks with an intense stare. "Go," she said in a tone that brooked no argument, waving them off. "Hide in the fields until the sun returns. We will find you once it is safe, and for the love of Olodumare and all that is righteous, stay out of sight."

The small group clutched at their children, bowing their heads gratefully as they ran off into the night on silent steps. "Come now, Vesper, we must hurry, time is short," she said, turning to face her.

"Do they not know what they are doing is wrong? How can they live with themselves?" she asked, looking at the twisted bodies of the fallen warriors.

"With the Sandawei, it is impossible to know. They are wicked and corrupt, more beast than man. But the truth is that they have always preferred to fight than work, and when their harvests are poor, they raid those who do what they cannot."

"We are all cut from the same cloth. Our struggles are the same as theirs. Why would they do that to their neighbors? To women and children just trying to eke out another day," asked Vesper, looking at them in disgust."

Magda shook her head, giving Vesper a sidelong glance as they moved on, returning to the shadows while quickening their pace. "The Sandawei were the first to discover the weave. They were the first people Olodumare created and gifted with power, and they think themselves above all others and see us as little more than animals. But from the beginning they were flawed, broken creatures, incapable of love and empathy, driven only by a lust for power, and so after a time Olodumare moved on, abandoning his original creations in favor of us."

Vesper balked, shaking her head. "Yes, but to steal someone's life, their freedom: it's monstrous, inhumane!"

"Yes, when Olodumare abandoned them they lost access to the weave, and in their hunger for power they looked too deep into the darkness beyond the veil of the weave, and what they found stole what little good was left in them."

Vesper's thoughts flew back to the gaping holes in the weave, those dark places that called to her, drawing her deep into the void when she was trying to find her mother among its vast tapestry. "What did they find?" she asked in a hushed tone.

Magda shrugged. "No one knows for sure, to do so would risk suffering the same fate, but it's one of the reasons that the Ose exist, the reason God gave us power. The chosen are meant to serve as a bulwark, to hold back what lies beyond the void."

"How are we supposed to protect—"

"Down!" screamed her aunt, slamming into her without warning and pushing her roughly aside, sending her careening down into the dirt, scraping her hands as she fell. Clenching her teeth at the pain, Vesper quickly rolled over, scanning the darkness for threats. She was about to spring to her feet when her aunt let out a haunting shriek, arching her back as a Sandawei spear pierced her chest, going clean through and coming out her back, spraying Vesper with flecks of warm blood and clotting on the dirt. For a moment she didn't believe it was real, that it was some sort of trick, but the pain etched on Magda's face brought the stark reality into place, and Vesper rushed to catch her, just as a Sandawei warrior emerged from the shadows, his demonic face splitting into a predatory grin as he stalked toward her with a hungry look in his cold eyes.

"No," she whispered, a lump forming in the pit of her stomach when the painted warrior stopped over her aunt's still form, planting his boot into her chest and brutally pulling his spear from her body with a sickening sound of bone and muscle tearing, a hollow rattle escaping her aunt's throat while blood spilled from her mouth which opened and closed in a silent scream.

The Sandawei warrior looked up from her aunt's still form, locking his horrid gaze on her, and Vesper scrambled back, fighting the urge to turn and run. Hefting his bloody spear he took a single step toward her, cocking his head like he was seeing her for the first time. Vesper knew she could jump away, vanishing along the lines of the tapestry to somewhere far away from this nightmare, and in the span of a single breath be somewhere safe... but if there was even a chance that her aunt was still alive, she wouldn't leave: she had to know.

The Sandawei came fully into the light as he stalked toward her, and Vesper's breath caught in her throat. He was different from the others. While his face was still marked with streaks of white paint, and the horns on the sides of his head were the same, he walked hunched over, moving more like a beast than a man, sniffing at her like a wild dog with the scent of prey in his nose. The strangest part of him was the blank, unblinking stare he gave her. Now that he was closer, she could see his pupils were covered with a strange milky film as if he were blind, but by the way he followed her, she was sure he knew exactly where she was. "Hush, hush, little Ose, don't cry," he began in an accent so thick she could hardly make out his words. "You are a fine djambe and you will fetch a fine price, more if you're undamaged. So come, come with Papa Jufari, and I promise you will be treated well in my care until you are sold."

Vesper swallowed hard, trying to keep the tremble from her voice. "No," she said, "you'll have to kill me."

"Oh, no no, that would be wasteful. You smells of good juju—raw, untouched. A fine price, a fine price we get for you. I will see you get a kind master," he said, sniffing at her again and then cocking his head, like something had just occurred to him. "Maybe even keep ya for me."

Scrambling to her feet without taking her eyes off him, Vesper stepped back on legs that felt like rubber, her entire body shaking so hard she had to put a trembling hand on the wall of the hut to keep from falling. "Please, just let me go," she said, shaking her head as tears rolled down her face.

"And give up such a prize, no, no. Come, come, time to be off." Like a hunting cat he pounced toward her, covering the distance between them in an instant. Vesper braced herself, flailing at his shoulders and face with feeble blows that only made his smile widen, batting aside her attacks, he laughed at her like a grinning hyena, slapping her with the back of his hand so hard she saw stars, her mouth filling with the taste of blood. Then as if she were a small child, he scooped her up like she weighed nothing, ignoring her feeble attacks, and throwing her over his shoulder.

Seeing her aunt laying unmoving in the dirt, Vesper fought like a cornered animal, flailing against his back and clawing at his skin, fighting with every ounce of her strength to break away or at least slip off him, but his grip was like iron, and his shoulders and back we're harder than stone, leaving Vesper's hands bloody and raw. "Please, we can't just leave her here," she begged, exhaustion making her limbs go weak.

"Oh, that flesh is nothing no more, cast off clay, the spark has returned to the weave, so no sense in crying, save your tears for the livin'."

She looked up at the sky to find the thread that was her aunt's life cut, dangling, her image dim. Vesper shrieked like her heart had been torn out, her middle feeling suddenly hollow. Her aunt had been her whole world, the one constant in her life... and now she was gone like she had never been, cut down trying to protect her. In that moment she stopped fighting against the Sandawei, her entire body falling limp as she stared at her aunt's corpse, trying to hold back the wave of guilt boiling up from her soul. This had been her fault. If only she had paid attention, had listened. Her aunt would still be here, to teach her about what she was meant to do, to teach her all the things her mother would have taught her... teach her about life.

"Time to go," said the Sandawei, pulling her mind away from the grief that threatened to crush her soul. Shifting her on his shoulders, he stood to his full height. "Papa Jufari take you home now." From the sheath on his hip he pulled out a bone dagger, bleached white by the sun and covered in strange circular symbols. The strange instrument was bent and twisted, looking like it had been gnawed on by some hungry beast, and was topped with black feathers and colored beads dangling from its hilt.

For a moment Vesper braced herself, thinking he was going to stab her with it, but instead he began to sing under his breath, his tone surprisingly soft yet deep. "You hold on tight now," he said as the light around them dimmed like the sun being eclipsed. A cold wind blew over her, raising gooseflesh, and making her teeth clatter, and without warning they were somewhere else, somewhere dark where even the sound of her breathing was muted, sounding far away.

She swore under her breath as she looked around, the village, the fire, even her aunt's body were all gone and she found herself along a dark cobblestone path that branched off into the dark. "Where are we," she asked, flinching at the hollow sound of her voice.

"Papa Jufari full of old tricks. He know the old ways, the way home that no one can see and no one follow, but don't worry, you stick close and you be safe, lots of stuff in the dark, best to stay on the path."

Taking a look around, Vesper had no idea where she was, but looking down at the monster of a man who had taken her she knew she had to get away. Calming herself, she tried to focus on the weave, intending to grab hold of the lines of Aṣẹ that connected all places and things and jump home to her aunt, to her people. But with a gasp she realized there was nothing there. There were no softly glowing threads, no plants to provide her with the power, only darkness, darkness and Papa Jufari, humming softly under his breath.

NINE

A VOICE IN THE DARK

Papa Jufari bounded along the dark cobblestone path, holding her tight over his shoulders with little effort. For the first little while of their journey, she had raged against her captor, thrashing about like a wild animal, gnashing her teeth against his flesh, but he ignored her ineffectual punches and kicks as if he were made of stone and not flesh and blood. When at last she had stopped fighting, the memory of what had happened hit her, and it no longer mattered where they were. She was numb inside and out, her mind a fog as the image of the spear piercing her aunt's breast replayed over and over in her brain. She wanted to scream, to shout, and she had tried, but something about this place, wherever it was, muted sound, so she remained silent turning the pain inward, and after a time Papa Jufari's bouncing gait, along with her exhaustion left her drifting in and out of consciousness, chasing the blissful escape of sleep that, for some reason, wouldn't come.

She was almost unconscious when a voice called to her, whispering her name over and over again, snapping her fully awake. Her senses were suddenly alive and she lifted her head, shifting on her captor's shoulders to get a better view of what was out there.

For a moment she felt a surge of hope, that somehow there was someone or something out there that was coming to help, but the longer she stared into the dark, hope faded, and she quickly realized there was little to see but barren gray soil that faded to an inky shadow not far beyond the cobblestone path they followed, and it wasn't long before what little hope she had found faded.

"You hear them calling," said Papa Jufari matter-of-factly, the sound of his voice making her flinch. "They is tryin' to trick you. If you go to them, go off the path, you'll lose your way, never to be seen again among the living."

"Then why come here, and where are you taking me?" asked Vesper, craning her neck to catch his eye. From the view from his shoulders, Vesper spied that they were coming to a crossroads of some kind, the path in front of them splitting into a V.

"I take you where I take you," said Jufari, stopping to inspect the path spread out before them. Shaking his head, he drew in a deep breath sniffing at the air like a hound, all the while holding her over his shoulder like she weighed nothing. With a snort he turned to look behind them and then forward again, his brow creased with worry while he mumbled in his guttural tongue under his breath.

"What's wrong?" she asked, trying to follow his gaze, straining to see what had unnerved him.

He gave her a milky-eyed glare, waving the bone dagger in front of them. "Something's following Papa Jufari. The air stinks somethin' foul."

Vesper wrinkled her nose, drawing in a lungful of the musty, stale air. It was odd. The air smelled of winter rain, cool and damp, but had just a hint of something foul, like meat that had been left out in the sun at the height of summer. "I don't smell anything," she said at last, not wanting to help him in the least.

"Papa Jufari got the gift," he said, running a finger along the side of his nose. "I can sniff out secrets of the universe; nothin' can hide from me, even here."

"And where exactly is here? I deserve some answers!" demanded

Vesper, raising her voice in anger, remembering that this man had killed her aunt and how many others.

Papa Jufari dropped her like a bale of wheat, giggling to himself while he looked down his nose at her. "I forget that you Ose know nothin' and less than nothin'," he said, waving the feather-capped dagger over her head, his voice intense. "Dis be the where the blind can see and God cannot, the place in between, where the universe is all stitched together."

Listening to his gibberish, Vesper couldn't help but roll her eyes. "I understand why my aunt didn't like you people. You talk in circles and you make no sense."

"That may be so, but if the Sandawei are so foolish, why is the Ose girl the prisoner and not me? No, no, I make sense to Papa Jufari, you people are—"

A booming crack of thunder echoed in the distance, accompanied by flashes of lightning that illuminated the barren landscape for a heartbeat. Vesper gasped, her blood running cold when she saw at last what darkness hid. Bounding to her feet, she immediately shuffled closer to Papa Jufari, her hatred for him forgotten. "Who are they? They can't be real, can they?" she asked, sucking in a nervous breath in a attempt to calm her nerves. "There were more than I could count."

Papa Jufari pursed his lips, nodding slowly. "They are very real," he said, eyeing her as if she should know. "Souls of the forgotten and forsaken. They watch, they wait."

Another flash of lightning brightened the sky once more, and she caught sight of them again. They were watching her with empty eyes that looked disturbingly similar to Papa Jufari's milky gaze: hundreds, thousands of listless souls, revenants standing and staring at them with a vacant hunger. "What are they waiting for, and why do they know my name," she asked, covering her ears to block out their whispers.

"No one knows," said Papa Jufari with a shrug, "but they have always been here, and they know the names of all who pass, calling them to damnation."

She shuddered, wrapping her arms around herself at the thought of being trapped here in this dismal place for all eternity, standing listlessly in the dark. "Can we go? I'll stop fighting you. I just want to be gone from this place," she said in a low voice, pushing the dark thoughts from her mind.

"No, I must deal with what is following us," he said, pointing to a rock at the center of the crossroads. "You shall sit there and not move until I return."

"You can't just leave me here. What happens if they come for me?" she blurted, pointing out to the barren fields, terrified at the thought of being alone in this dismal place, her breathing coming faster while fear gripped at her heart. The last thing she wanted was to be sold off like an animal, but the idea of being trapped forever terrified her even more.

"Papa Jufari will hide you from prying eyes, those of the living anyway," he said, passing the bone dagger over her head "As for the dead, as long as you stay on the path, they cannot harm you."

"What if you don't come back?" she said, plopping down on the hard, makeshift seat.

"I am sure to return, but if I don't, well, that's your problem, not mine," he said with a cackle, his face twisting with amusement.

Shaking in terror, she pulled her knees in close, folding in on herself as she watched him run back the way they came, her gaze locked on the path long after he had vanished from her view. With him gone it seemed darker, colder, and the whispers calling to her more frantic. Vesper knew she should run while she had the chance and find some way to make it out of here and back home. She imagined following the cobblestone path would be dangerous, but her alternative would be to wait for Jufari... if he ever came back, and even if he did, what would be her fate? To be sold off like cattle to some Roman, or worse, Jufari would keep her for himself, whatever that meant. No, she wouldn't be anyone's slave. She would rather face fear and death going back the way they came even if it meant her life.

Squaring her shoulders, she straightened her dress and stood, determined to make it home, or die trying. Setting off the way they came, it occurred to her that she would have to find a way to avoid Jufari as the last thing she wanted was to be caught by him along the path and waste her opportunity. To survive she would have to risk leaving the road, and she was sure just going off a few feet while keeping sight of the road would be a reasonable risk.

"Leaving the road would be foolish," said a voice from darkness that made her jump out of her skin. "Jufari is many things, foolish even, but in this he is right. Stay on the path if you wish to avoid an eternity of damnation."

"Who's there?" said Vesper, her heart beating like a drum as she turned in place, trying to look everywhere at once. Scanning the darkness she thought for a moment that her mind was playing tricks on her, that somehow the echo of her footfalls on the cobblestone path along with the distant thunder had made her hear something that wasn't there. She waited for an answer, her shoulders hunched and stiff while she stood at alert, but there was nothing, no voice, no movement, and slowly the tension faded, leaving her standing in the middle of the road with her muscles weak like she had spent all day working under the hot sun.

Her breathing had just returned to normal when the voice spoke again, louder this time, still coming from everywhere at once. "Don't you know me? I know you very well... Vesper."

Cold beads of sweat formed on her temples and her mouth went dry. There was something about the voice, something familiar: she had heard it before but she couldn't place it. "Should I?" she asked, turning in place, licking her lips, a hollow void growing in the pit of her stomach.

"Of course. I've been with you, always, from the moment you came into the world, to this very day."

"I'm not some fool!" shouted Vesper. "It's like Jufari said, you're just trying to trick me."

"Just the opposite," said the voice, louder now, sounding more confident with each word. "I am here to offer you salvation, to save you."

"Leave me be," she said. Grinding her teeth in frustration, she fought the urge to give up and walk into the darkness. She was tired of being powerless, of being trapped in this horrible place, made worse now that she was being taunted by something she couldn't see or even understand. Not knowing what else to do, she ran, gingerly moving down the path in the direction she last saw Jufari, hoping her legs would carry her far away from the voice. After the first few steps, she thought she had succeeded and it had gone or at the least that she had imagined the whole thing.

"Finding Jufari is not the answer!" snapped the voice, its intensity stopping Vesper in her tracks. "Unless we kill him, he will do to you the terrible things men do to women, and when he tires of you, he will sell you to some Roman who will do the same, or worse. And it will go on from one master to another until you are used up, with nothing left to give. It's a terrible life, one that I can save you from."

"How?" said Vesper, truly terrified now. The voice felt like it was thrumming through her bones now, itching like ants crawling over her skin.

"We can escape here together," said the voice. "I can help you... if you help me."

"The only thing I want is to go home."

The voice paused, seeming to shift closer, like it was whispering a secret in her ear. "Then we want the same thing. I wish to be free of this place, just like you. I want to go home, to be with those I love. I want to see the sun rise, to feel its heat on my face."

Vesper shivered at the hunger of the voice, the intensity. "Papa Jufari said that this place is home to the forsaken. Why should I help you, for all I know you're some sort of vile spirit, something evil that needs to be kept hidden away from the world."

The voice seemed to pull back, going from a whisper to an ear-piercing wail that made her flinch. "You dare speak to me this way! How can you be so ungrateful for all that I have done for you. I have known you all the days of your life. I carried you in my belly, endured the suffering of birthing you into this world. I nurtured you at my breast! The Aṣẹ that marks your skin, the power you have to touch the world, it all comes from me!"

"That's impossible, you're dead," said Vesper, backing to the edge of the path, her mind reeling at the possibility. "Magda, my aunt... she told me you were dead, gone."

"My sister was a fool," said the voice, no longer just a voice but a physical presence, washing over her like a stinking wind, its stinging heat blistering her skin. "She never understood the power we have. She never understood the game, and never understood what had to be done to win."

Vesper's mind raced back to the dream she had on the first day she touched her power, to the memory of a woman sitting across from her taunting her to play a game that changed every time she looked away from the board. The girl had been as beautiful as her aunt had been intelligent. "Lillith?" she said, hesitating, her voice little more than a croak. "Mother?"

The wind stilled, and Vesper felt the voice move in close once again, circling her like a warm embrace, and when it spoke, it was full of joy and love. "Yes, my gift to the world, my evening star, my Vesper... at last we are together: at last we will be one."

TEN

MOTHER AND DAUGHTER

Vesper's mother had died not long after she was born, and she knew her only through the stories told to her by Magda and her father. Stories that made her out to be more like a goddess of myth and legend than a woman of flesh and blood. As a result, to Vesper she was larger than life. A great warrior who held their countless enemies at bay with her skill and cunning and powerful djambe that bent the universe to her will—perfect, without flaws. But the voice echoing all around her sounded nothing like that. Lillith's words tumbled from the darkness with a very mortal mix of joy and sadness, love and loss. "My child look at you. I am filled with such pride. You are so beautiful, so strong. I am filled with sadness for every day that I've missed."

"Father, Magda, they told me you were dead," repeated Vesper, blowing out her cheeks, trying to hold back hot tears, to hold back the well of emotion bubbling up inside her that threatened to leave her a blubbering mess. Magda, Olodumare protect her soul, had done her best to raise her, protect her, and from now to the end of her days, she would hold her memory dear to her heart, but she was not her mother.

"Not dead... just lost, but I am with you now. I love you, and once we escape from this place, I promise I'll never leave your side ever again."

To hear her mother say that she loved her, that she was proud of who she had become made her heart sing. It made her want to spin in place and shout with joy. But she couldn't, not here, not while they were in so much danger. Vesper took a deep breath to steady herself, to calm the torrent of laughter and tears that threatened to overwhelm her, when at last she felt she was ready, she squared her shoulders, cleaning her face. "What must I do to get us out of here... and away from Jufari?"

Lillith was silent for a few moments, and Vesper thought she had said something wrong, but when her mother spoke at last, her tone was grim. "There is no other way; we must kill him," began Lillith, "and use his dying spirit to snap us back to where this journey began."

Vesper stifled a gasp, worry bubbling up in her stomach. "I'm not like you, Mother. Until earlier tonight I had never touched a weapon, and I only used the weave for the first time yesterday."

"My sister has truly failed in her duty; what was she doing with you?" said Lillith with some heat in her voice. "By the time we were your age we had already fought and bled for our people: we were seasoned warriors."

"I'm sorry," said Vesper, bowing her head while wringing her hands. "I did my—"

"It is not your fault, Daughter. Magda was always too cautious, always afraid of her own shadow."

Vesper let out a breath she hadn't realized she was holding, tension draining from her shoulders. "So what do we do?"

"A dangerous thing. If you are brave enough," said Lillith, speaking slowly.

"Anything! I'm not afraid!"

"Good. This will be difficult, but together we will succeed. I am sure of it."

"Tell me," said Vesper, bouncing with anticipation, her heart racing.

"I will mount you, and we shall combine our spirit and flesh into one being. Once we are together, I will be in control, and will use everything I know, all of my power to have revenge on this murder, and hopefully get us home."

Vesper had heard of such superstitions, of calling powerful spirits known as Loa with offerings or sacrifice. The hope would be that the netherworld being would do you some favor, or grant you some boon, and in rare cases, do as her mother had said, to join spirit to flesh and grant the summoner great power for a short time. "Magda said the Loa were not real, that they were made up by charlatans to trick the gullible."

"Yes... and no," said her mother, sounding like she was searching for her words. "Some pretend that the Loa have mounted them, hoping to curry favor with the foolish, but the vodun are very real; some are kind, others very dangerous, but all are hungry to join their spirit with a summoner's body, always wanting more, but this won't be the same. I am not some distant spirit wanting a taste of flesh: we are kin, and I will return control to you once we are safe."

"How do I... I mean do I have to do something? How does it work," asked Vesper, rubbing her arms and feeling foolish.

Vesper had the impression, once again, of the voice coming closer, its whisper sending a chill over her scalp like fingers were touching her skin. "You must call to me, call on my power, invite me in, so to speak... and there must be an offering," said Lillith. "Some part of you given freely, blood, or a bit of hair... but the blood works best."

"I don't have anything to cut—" she said, looking around for something that would do the job.

"The rock, your hand, quickly," snapped her mother. "Jufari returns."

"What? How do you—? I mean how can you see anything in this gloom," she said, racing back along the path to the crossroad, to where the Sandawei had left her.

"It was my trick that sent him away," said Lillith, "and now he will return soon. We must hurry. I will give you the words that must be said to summon me."

The darkness became a blur as she pumped her legs as quickly as they would take her, absorbing her mother's words for the summoning. Vesper arrived at the rock and quickly fell to her knees, gasping for breath while she hunted for an edge sharp enough to do what had to be done.

"You think Papa Jufari be a fool!" Vesper cringed, quickly glancing over her shoulder to find the Sandawei charging toward her, the strange animal horns on the sides of his head bouncing wildly, his face a mask of rage. "You try and trick me, no, no."

Seeing him so close, Vesper rushed to slice open her hand on the jagged stone, only to squeal when Jufari yanked her back by her hair, throwing her bodily through the air like a child's toy. The air was blasted from her lungs when she landed on her back a few feet away, skidding along the cobblestones until she came to a grinding halt, arching her back and rolling onto her side in a vain attempt to escape the pain.

She opened her eyes to find him towering above her, frothing at the mouth. "I was trying to be good to you, to show you some kindness, but now, I'm gonna go back, kill the rest of your people as punishment for your disrespect. Then I'm gonna sell you to the worst of the worst, so you gonna spend the rest of your days wishing for the kindness of Papa Jufari."

"Mother... please!" she rasped through the hurt, her back and head throbbing.

Jufari's lips twisted into a cruel smile and he shook his head. "Call to your ancestors all you want, girl," he began, slapping her with the back of his hand, sending her reeling from the blow, seeing stars. "No one here but you an' me," he continued, Vesper tasting blood in her mouth when he slapped her again, harder this time.

Spots appeared in the corners of her eyes as she fought to stay conscious. Her face and back were on fire, pulsing with more pain than she had ever known. Vesper wanted nothing more than to give up, to fall into the blissful release of death and leave the world behind, and she almost did; it felt easy in this place. But then she remembered suffering on her aunt's face as Jufari's spear ripped through her chest, and she pictured him doing that to the people of her village—mothers, fathers, children not old enough to understand hate. Every last one of them would be killed or enslaved by this monster. And her mother, who she had just found, would be trapped here forever with the rest of the damned. "No!" she shouted. "I'll kill you first!" Jufari pulled back to strike her again and she did the only thing she could think of. Rolling onto her side, she grabbed at his leg, locking her teeth onto his ankle with all her might.

Jufari's eyes shot open, a vile screech spilling from his throat as he reached down to tear her off of him. Vesper railed against him, adrenaline giving her the strength to hold on to his leg for dear life and to keep biting.

"Enough!" he shouted, lifting her bodily by the hair once more and pulling hard enough that Vesper had to let go or risk losing her teeth. Jufari pulled her close, and she retched in disgust at his rancid breath. "You Ose think you still rule Africa, that you have power, but you are nothin' more than Roman lapdogs begging for scraps at your master's table. But soon you will be no more, forgotten like you never was, and the Sandawei will rule once again."

Looking into Papa Jufari's milky gaze, Vesper squeezed her eyes shut, using all her strength to hold herself up so that her hair wouldn't tear away from her scalp. "You must be brave," whispered Lillith in her ear. "Be brave for me, for all those that have fallen, be brave for Magda."

Vesper had never been brave; she never had to be. Magda had sheltered her, protected her from the world. "I'll try," she whispered through the shooting pain in her scalp.

Papa Jufari narrowed his milky gaze, glancing around in confusion. "Who you speakin' to? Do you be foolish enough to answer the damned," he said, throwing his head back with a mocking laugh.

Seeing that his eye's milky gaze was not on her, Vesper desperately lunged for the bone-handled dagger on his hip, needles of sharp pain exploding from her skull when all her weight was suddenly supported by her hair. With a growl she tore the weapon from the sheath on his hip, slashing clumsily and cutting deep into his arm.

Jufari let go with a surprised yelp, and she fell at his feet in a heap, brandishing the blade in front of her like a shield while she scurried back. "You're the only one here who is damned."

"You think this be somethin'," he said, frowning at the cut on his arm with a shrug. "This is nothin', you think that blade can hurt Papa Jufari, no, no. Fool Ose, I gonna take your scalp. You can still be pretty without that mess you call hair. Yes, pretty, pretty."

Vesper drew in a shuddering breath, trying to calm her fear as he stalked closer to her with a feral grin on his face. "It's not for you," she said, flipping the blade and plunging it into her palm, beginning the chant her mother had taught her only moments before. "Come to me, Lillith."

In front of her Jufari stopped cold, his milky eyes going wide with shock. "No! Foolish Ose, you will kill us both!" he shouted, stumbling back, showing the whites of his palms. "Damnation, eternal damnation!"

Vesper continued, pumping her closed fist above her head, her life blood running down her arm and spilling on the cobblestones before vanishing like rain on parched earth. "Grant me your boon so that I may vanquish my enemies. I offer my blood, my body... my life." Her muscles tensed and her body tingled as a blast of icy cold made her stagger. In front of her a flickering shadow surged toward her, its shape twisting and bending in a way that made her stomach heave. For a heartbeat it grew to an immense size, a mountain of darkness that encompassed everything she could see, looking like it could devour that world. An instant later it was smaller than a gnat, so tiny and feeble that she could crush it with a finger. The shadow came closer and she recoiled, only to freeze in place when it passed into her palm.

"I am with you, Daughter," said Lillith, appearing to stand in front of her, her words no longer a whisper but strong and clear. Vesper knew her immediately. They shared the same dark, mysterious eyes; high cheekbones; and smooth, unblemished skin. But Lillith was taller with full lips and a high forehead, her hair plaited in a long braid that ran down her back. "And now it's time to make this fool suffer for his arrogance. Are you ready? Do you accept me?"

Vesper nodded, embracing her, and for a moment she was filled with the knowledge of Aṣẹ, of true power to change the universe, her mind overflowing with martial skills beyond anything she had ever imagined. Terrifying rituals that called on powers too alien to behold flooded her being, leaving her gasping for air at the horror of it all... and then just as quickly, it was gone, vanished from her mind like it never was. Vesper staggered, losing her balance and falling toward the cobblestone path. In a panic she tried to raise her arms to catch herself, to not fall on her face, but to her shock, her arms wouldn't respond, and her legs moved without her accord to keep her upright... and she was suddenly a passenger in her own body. She watched herself as if through an open window, yet still able to smell the chalky dry air, to feel the cool dampness, or even to taste the blood in her mouth from when Jufari had hit her. But when she tried to move her limbs it felt like she was trying to pull herself up with a rope covered in grease, and no matter how much she tried, she couldn't get a grip.

"Stop fighting me, it only makes it more difficult," said Lillith in a voice that sounded oddly like her own.

"Are you still in there, fool Ose, or has this roho, this vile spirit pushed you out all the way," said Jufari, having regained his composure and waving his arms in a twisted way that made it look like he was writing something in the air. "No matter, after Jufari finishes with you, only ash will remain."

"What does he mean?" said Vesper, her voice now sounding like the whisper, the sense of falling growing stronger.

"Don't listen to him," said Lillith. "He knows he is about to pay the price for his sins, to die for his crimes."

A gale-force wind slammed into her chest and Vesper was hurled back, tumbling end over end until she had no idea which way was up, and which was down. "Where am I?" she croaked, at last coming to a halt and finding herself off the cobblestone path, her body little more than a transparent shade that faded with each passing moment, like a shadow when the sun hid behind the clouds. A howling wind filled her ear and, in the distance, she could see them, hear them. The wailing shades of the damned calling to her with voices full of rage, begging for her to join their vile song. Vesper shuddered, turning away, afraid of what she might become if she went to them.

Jufari's mad cackle pulled her attention away from the damned, turning, she saw him further down the cobblestone path, hurling spears made of shadow at a girl who wore her face and shouted with her voice. Vesper opened her mouth to scream and shout, but there was nothing but a soft whisper, and she realized that now she was the spirit, the ghost, and the girl in the distance was who she once was. She was detached from her body, the flesh no longer under her control. This was not what her mother had told her would happen, and even in the tales her aunt had told her, the Loa shared their power, the spirit and the flesh working together as one. But instead, she had been cast out, abandoned to walk in this dark place alone, to spend eternity among the damned. Her mother had lied...

Vesper watched them fight as if the world had slowed, their movements crawling almost to a halt. Furthermore, she could see every detail, each breath, every bead of sweat rolling down their skin. Jufari snapped forward, somehow weaving together strands of shadow from this place to create a razor-tipped spear that he hurled with deadly precision, the dark weapon somehow crawling through the air ever so slowly, only to blink in confusion when the deadly weapon stopped a hairsbreadth from her physical form, held in place by some unseen force.

"All this power at your fingertips, Jufari," said Lillith in a mocking tone, laughing with Vesper's voice, smiling with her face, "and you use it to make a spear of all things... a piece of wood topped with a bit of metal. Are you so weak minded, so simple? This is why we have defeated the Sandawei at every turn. You lack the imagination, the drive, even the will to rule. Your people are pathetic, and after I am done tearing you limb from limb, I will return to the world reborn, young and strong once more to finish what I started. I will make all of Africa fertile using the rotting corpses of your people, the Romans, too, and with time we will regain all that we've lost... the Ose empire will be whole once more."

"I will never let you escape this place, Demon!" shouted Jufari, lashing out again, this time coming at her with twin swords of flickering shadow, slashing wildly in a mad frenzy. Lillith watched him, unmoving, unfazed, untouched as the blades simply passed through her.

"As if you have a choice, Jufari," said Lillith, drawing together strands of darkness like he had done, but faster, and on a far grander scale, the sky above them echoing with thunder and lightning. "Nothing will stop me this time, not you, not mercy or love, not even family." The Sandawei's milky eyes went wide with shock when torrents of lightning exploded from the clouds and crooked arcs of blue bolts fell around them like rain. Vesper smiled when a crooked finger of cobalt slammed into Jufari, his every muscle tensing as the energy coursed through him, throwing the wretched man through the air and far away from Lillith. He landed with a grunt a grunt, thick tendrils of smoke drifting up from him while he twisted in agony.

Sensing her chance, Vesper rushed forward, circling her mother like a typhoon, desperately searching for a way back in.

"Are you still there, my daughter?" said Lillith, raising an eyebrow. "I see you have my strength; most spirits would have fled or faded by now... especially here among the damned."

Vesper wanted to rail against her, to pound her fists into her chest, but she was nothing more than the wisp of a shadow, her words little more than whispers. "Why would you do this? You said we could return together."

"I'm sorry I had to deceive you, Vesper," she began, stalking toward Jufari, drawing in more of the dark energy that permeated this place, "but after a lifetime trapped with the damned..."

"You would betray those you love," said Vesper, still not believing that her own mother had selfishly cast her aside and condemned her to an eternity in this wretched place.

Lillith came to a halt over the fallen Sandawei, and she continued, "Yes. I love you with all my heart, but I must be hard now, for the greater good, no matter the cost."

"So what happens now?" asked Vesper, her mind racing as to how she could end this nightmare and simply be herself again. "What will you do? What will become of me?"

"I will begin by ending this fool's life and riding his dying spirit back to the land of the living," she said, raising a hand to the sky, booming flashes of lightning streaking across the heavens. "As for you, my child, if you have not begun already, you will fade away until you are nothing more than pale shadow of what you once were. But don't worry, it will be a kindness. With time, you will forget everyone and everything, and you will spend your days like the rest of the damned, wailing in sorrow for a life you can no longer remember."

Vesper's gaze snapped to the infinite number of pale souls scattered across the barren landscape, at last understanding their wailing song. They cried out in agony for lives forgotten, hungry for even a single memory of what was lost. A flash of color in the corner of her eye drew her attention to the scene before. Lillith stood with her hand raised high about to call down the wrath of the almighty. At her feet the fallen Sandawei spat vile words of hatred, defiant to the end. Vesper's attention was riveted to her mother's hand, her hand, her blood was still dripping down onto the cobblestone road. To Vesper's amazement, the spots of blood glowed ever so softly when they landed, driving back the dark for just a moment so that she could see flecks of ochre and amber in the cobblestones that filled the path. "My blood, it was her way in, and it was filled with power, like the lily from her aunt's garden, power enough to drive away the shadow," she said to herself, reaching out to touch the trickle of crimson.

Lillith saw her too late, her eyes going wide as she tried to pull away. The instant Vesper touched the blood, a deafening roar filled her ear as she reentered her body. Fighting her mother for control was like trying to tame a wild beast, a lion who fought against her at every turn. In desperation Vesper pushed with every ounce of her will until she felt the familiar weight of her limbs, the rush of air filling her lungs... and something more. For the second time today she felt the duality. She wasn't alone, and her mind was filled with memories of places she'd never been, the faces of people she'd never known flashed before her eyes. For a moment she was back in her dream in the tent, looking at it all from a different perspective, staring into her Aunt Magda's younger face, arguing that she should play the game. Her perspective shifted again, and now she was next to a Roman she had never met yet somehow knew intimately: Marcus Aurelius, caesar of Rome lay next to her, his strong arm draped over her.

"You arrogant child," shouted her mother, somehow slamming the door to her memories shut. "Why couldn't you be like the other shades in this place and just fade away? Don't you understand, I'm doing this to make the world a better place!"

Lillith pushed harder against her, and Vesper felt like she was slipping away again, staggering, desperately fighting for control. Behind the wall her mother had put up, Vesper could sense an immense burning hatred for the world, and a hunger for vengeance that she couldn't understand. "Killing people like Jufari is one thing, but what about the innocents, the men and women who don't go to war, who toil the land and tend the home, the children, and for what? Revenge? Power?"

"Look at him," said Lillith, pointing to Jufari. "Do you think his children will be kind and loving beacons of humanity... or will they be monsters and slavers like him. No its best to exterminate them now, remove their seed from the world before it grows into something foul."

"Then you're no better than him," she shouted as she hung on for dear life, all the while hunting for the spark of energy she had seen in her blood only moments before, the light in her that could stand in the darkness.

"If that's the way you feel, then Magda truly failed me, and you are no daughter of mine," she spat.

Vesper could feel Lillith drawing in torrents of dark energy, weaving it together until she sensed a cage forming around her mind and spirit. From the brief moments they had shared memories, she knew it was a trap that would make her a prisoner in her own body. Not really knowing how, she fled, slipping out of the dark cage just as the door slammed shut, twisting and turning through the corridors of her mind until she found herself hiding in the dark recess of memories long forgotten, leaving control to Lillith, but not daring to leave her body again. Lost among flashes of distant days long forgotten, she had a moment of respite. She saw herself clambering along the limbs of the great baobab tree she knew so well and watched fondly of her days playing with the other village children near its massive roots. A wave of comfort washed over her when the sound of her father's voice bubbled up into her consciousness, his deep voice gently easing her to sleep night after night. Her sister's round face came unbidden to her and suddenly they lay together in the soft grass looking up at the stars, dreaming of a future far away from their small part of the world.

"Sister?" whispered Vesper, having a moment of clarity, understanding at last that they were sharing much more than the body, but consciousness as well. She wasn't in her own mind... but somehow in Lillith's. It was all laid out before her. Somehow her mother's memories were mixed with her own, every skill, hope, and dream was laid bare. She only had to reach out and experience it. Vesper finally understood what had to be done. Knowing her mother was distracted, Vesper took advantage of her skill, drawing deep from the well of power that coursed through her veins. Her mother's memories had shown her that blood had more power than any plant, any tree, but it came at a price, a deadly one... but she would do what she had to. She only hoped she could live with herself afterward.

ELEVEN

DJAMBE

Vesper rushed from the dark corners of Lillith's mind, channeling a torrent of power through her soul so bright it made the sun look dim by comparison. Returning to the forefront of their combined consciousnesses, she was shocked to find that Jufari had somehow recovered, and now the two of them were locked in a titanic struggle. Lillith hurling cobalt bolts of lightning that arced wildly in all directions after being deflected by a shield Jufari just barely pulled together from wisps of shadow.

"That is enough, Mother," said Vesper, feeling strangely calm, floating in a well of power.

"Vesper... again, h-how," she stammered, her attacks against Jufari suddenly forgotten. "It doesn't matter, I will—"

"You will do nothing, Mother," said Vesper, using Lillith's own knowledge that now filled her mind to wrest control of her limbs. Grasping at the threads of dark energy Lillith had been using, she combined it with the brilliant torrent of power that, until now, lay dormant in her own blood. With a finesse she didn't know she had, Vesper poured the energy through the image of the baobab tree that Magda had tattooed on her chest, using it as a focus for the raw power she was holding. "Your time was over long ago, Mother. You failed, you died. And I won't let you destroy my life the way you did yours."

"Foolish girl! Don't you think I've planned for everything, every contingency, even death?" said Lillith. "Your life is my life. The only reason you exist is because I willed you into existence. Through you and the others, I will have all the time I need."

"Others?" she said, her brows coming together.

"It does not matter. You're not real, just bits of bone and blood I weaved together for my purposes."

Vesper hesitated, stung by her mother's words, and control of her limbs slipped once more, her arms falling limp, legs wobbling like they were made of rubber. In front of her, Papa Jufari narrowed his milky gaze, looking for some tricks to why she had stopped attacking and now stood stock still, his chest heaving like he had just run a race.

"No!" shouted Vesper, the words exploding from her lips and echoing across the barren plane. "I'm real and don't care what your plans were for me or anyone else. It's my life, and now I'm taking it back!" Drinking in from the well of power she had created, Vesper drew on the knowledge she had found in Lillith's mind, weaving together strands of light and dark, layering the energy of life and death into an impenetrable weave to bind the vile creature that was once her mother, driving her consciousness behind an impassable wall that would hold her for all time, a prison deep within Vesper's mind, body, and soul.

"What are you doing!" shouted Lillith, her voice fading with each passing moment, muted by the forming barrier that held her in place. "What is this? Let me out! Let me go!" In front of her, Jufari smiled to himself, beads of sweat leaving rivulets down his white-painted face.

She staggered when her mother threw her will against the barrier, pounding at the cage with all her strength, hunting for weakness like a cornered rat scrambling for some way out. Drawing deeper, Vesper reinforced the prison, building layer after layer until her mother's blows were little more than an annoyance, her screams only a faint buzzing.

Seeing her distracted, Jufari drew back his arm, and a shadowy spear appeared in his hand, his milky gaze hard and unblinking. Like a lion springing from the tall grass, his arm snapped forward, aiming the dark weapon for her chest.

Vesper saw it all happening, her attention never wavering from the treacherous Sandawei's face despite her internal battle with her mother. She saw the spear released and drew once more on the well of knowledge and experience she had taken from Lillith's mind. With a flick of her wrist she caught the simple weapon in thin strands of power, and then did the same thing to Papa Jufari, holding them both in place. "My mother was right," she said to herself as much to the wide-eyed Jufari, who trembled in front of her. "All your supposed power, and this is the best you can do."

The Sandawei raised his chin, giving her a defiant look while he struggled against the thin tendrils of power holding him in place. "It was good enough for your protector, for the woman I killed when I took you!"

At the mention of her aunt, something within her snapped, and with a fierce growl, Vesper lifted him off the ground while snapping her palm open, causing his arms and legs to splay wide like they were being pulled in all directions. "Her name was Magda," said Vesper through gritted teeth, pulling harder. She watched with grim satisfaction as his body trembled, every muscle shaking, his bones and tendons cracking. "And she was a good person, kind and loving. And she deserved better than to die by your hand."

Despite the agony etched on his face, a grim cackle escaped from Jufari's throat. "A filthy Ose witch like her," he said with a strained voice. "She deserved it... in fact... if I look, I'm sure she... if you look... she is out there, standing with the rest of the damned."

"You'll join her soon enough," said Vesper, wrenching control of the shadowy spear he had created, flipping it around and driving its razor-sharp tip every so slowly into Jufari's heaving chest, sending thin rivulets of blood rolling down his sides.

Jufari's eyes went wide with disbelief when the dark weapon

pierced his skin, his lips twisting into a horrible grimace while the tip inched ever so slowly through breastbone. "If you kill me, you will damn yourself to this place," he screamed, "but I can take you home... set you free."

"I know you lie. And I know the way home lies through your death," she said, closing her fist, pouring all of her anger and hurt through the spear, using it as a beacon for every ounce of rage in her heart.

"No!" shouted Jufari, wildly shaking his head. "The Loa that rides you will never let you go now that it has a taste of you. It will—" The Sandawei let out a bloodcurdling scream that turned into a sickening wet rattle when the spear at last ripped through his chest, plunging past bone and flesh like it was papyrus.

"It's not enough," whispered Vesper, her anger raging as images of Magda's death played again and again in her mind. With a roar she wove more threads of power into the floating body, light and dark, fire and ice. With a final surge she separated the Sandawei into his basic elements, banishing his soul to live among the damned, while draining every ounce of blood. The rest she unleashed her wrath, burning it until all that was left was ash floating on the wind, flesh and bone transformed into its purest essence, before letting it drift away in the dark until nothing was left. When it was at last done, she let out a trembling breath that she didn't know she was holding, her entire body shivering with exhaustion as she fell to her knees with her head bowed, tears rolling down her cheeks.

She wasn't sure how long she sat there in the dark, but when she came to her senses, her entire body was numb from cold, and her legs were tingling from having fallen asleep. Somewhere in the back of her mind, her mother was still there. She could feel the faint buzz that was Lillith, raging against the walls of the prison Vesper had created, hunting for some way to escape, waiting to take control once more.

"Time to go home," said Vesper, her eyes locked on what was left of Jufari, a perfectly smooth crimson orb that floated in front of her.

Standing on trembling legs, she looked back and forth along the cobblestone path and pressed her lips together, doubt bubbling in her stomach. When she had been battling for control with Lillith, the knowledge her mother possessed flowed freely into her mind, but now that she had locked her away, it felt distant, like she was trying to remember something she had learned long ago. For a moment she was tempted to weaken the prison that separated them. It would have been easy enough to access the knowledge of the way home from Lillith's mind directly, but she wasn't sure if she could control her, and the last thing she wanted to do was face her mother again in her exhausted state. Looking down at the ash that was once Papa Jufari, it came back to her in fits and starts and she began the ritual that would take her home. Raising a hand over her head she squeezed hard, opening up the cut that was there. Sucking in a deep breath she began, drawing on the twin streams of power, some from her own blood, some from his, and more from the dark depths of this place. In a rush she continued, wanting this to be over quickly.

The cobblestone path remained eerily silent, and for a moment Vesper thought she had made a mistake and failed to do the ritual properly, but in the span of a single breath a hot fetid wind blew across the barren plane, and she sensed that the new Loa was present.

Wrapping it in her power, she commanded it, dominating it to her will so that it would lead her home. The cobblestone path began to glow with an amber light, and she could see a faint ghostly outline of Jufari, leading her back the way they had come, beckoning that she should follow, his face a mask of hatred, even in death.

Following the fallen Sandawei's spirit down the dark path, she was struck by the absurdity of it all. Jufari had never met her or anyone in her family, yet he hated her and all of the Ose even to the detriment of his own life. His hate had been his doom. Vesper's life had been upended because of some forgotten wrong lost to the annals of time, all that anger and violence for nothing. Nothing had changed except that her world was smaller. Now she and her people, if there were any left, would have to rebuild from the ashes. She only prayed that she would be strong enough. She had gained power at a terrible price, more power than she ever imagined having. As if thinking of her made her stronger. Vesper clutched her head, despair washing over her as she felt like a spike had been driven into her skull. Lillith raged in the back of her mind, fighting to escape the prison Vesper had created. While the pain ran through her, she worried that she would not be able to contain her mother's corruption, or worse, that given time, she would fall to the same evils. She was about to give in to despair when she remembered Magda's sacrifice. Her aunt had taken Jufari's spear to the chest so that Vesper could live... she couldn't fail her: she wouldn't.

Gathering her will, Vesper clenched her teeth and pushed back against Lillith's onslaught, bringing it to heel. This was her body and mind, her spirit, and she would not lose control of it ever again. Within moments the pain returned to the faint buzz it had been before. Getting to her feet, Vesper let out a shaking breath, knowing now that each day would be a struggle, but if she could hold back Lillith's rage, she could turn her mother's evil into a force for good. Setting off after the dark spirit, she quickened her pace, a smile creasing her face when she understood at last feeling that something good had come from all of this. She would spend the rest of her days making the world a better place. She would do the one thing that would make her people great again... she would give them hope, and for now, she prayed it would be enough.

EPILOGUE

The sun was a thin disk slowly descending over the horizon, casting the training grounds in a shimmering haze of amber and long shadows. The dusty square on the outskirts of the village was mostly empty now, with most of the students and trainers having had the good sense to go home to enjoy a well-deserved supper and prepare for sleep, but she did her best to avoid sleep now.

Vesper jumped back, every muscle straining as she sucked in her stomach to avoid a vicious jab from Kehinde's blunted training spear. Stumbling awkwardly, she twisted and turned trying to recover her balance while at the same time trying to avoid the tall man's long reach and relentless attacks. Seeing that Vesper was barely keeping to her feet, he changed tactics, whipping the long weapon low in wide circles, trying to knock her feet from under her. Thinking quickly, Vesper shifted her weight onto her back foot and parried the wild attack, spinning her own spear like a whirlwind to deflect the long weapon, then seeing an opening, she charged forward, forcing Kehinde on his heels with a series of quick feints aimed at his head. Undeterred, he danced back, neck and shoulders swaying like a cobra so that Vesper only caught air with her strikes.

"Am I too handsome?" said Kehinde with a smile, lazily knocking Vesper's spear wide before coming in again, attacking high and then low with a series of blindingly fast jabs with the spear.

Vesper growled, ducking low to avoid a swing and then retreated to avoid losing her head. "You have the face of an oxen, so you have little to lose." She laughed, goading him on while conserving her own strength, hoping to beat him by wearing him out.

Kehinde and his men were awǫn aabo, warriors and protectors rarely seen in the village. Men who spent most of their time scouting the wilds around the village for threats and keeping those working the fields safe, a task they had failed on that fateful night so many months ago. They had found Vesper near dawn, draped over her aunt's body, shielding it from a pack of hyenas that had been sniffing at the smell of dead flesh, hungrily circling in closer with every moment that passed. The tall, wiry man had fallen to his knees in despair when he realized who Vesper was protecting, and why, cursing himself and his men at what had happened. He had promised then and there that he would never fail her or their people again, that he would do everything in his power to protect and to train her to the best of his ability.

True to his word, they had begun training the very next day. While Vesper had expected to learn about Aṣẹ and the nature of power, about the things her aunt had started teaching, Kehinde knew nothing of those things, so he taught her what he knew: the spear and shield, sword and fist.

"Pay attention," he snapped, stopping his blunt spear only a hairsbreadth from her face.

"Sorry, Mwalimu," she said, cursing at herself, angry that she had become lost in thought, leaving herself open. With a deft twist of of her spear she knocked the other weapon aside, crouching once again to the starting position she knew so well. "It won't happen again."

The tall, wiry man stood to his full height, waving her off. "You call me teacher, but I am not sure if I am actually teaching you anything," he began, speaking slowly, like a man who rarely spoke. "One moment you fight better than any awọn aabo I have ever seen, and I would be honored to have you among my men, and the next you behave as the young girl you are, barely able to hold your spear."

Vesper let the spear fall to her side, pressing her lips together in a thin line. "I just get tired, Mwalimu," she lied, not able to meet his gaze. How could she possibly explain that every thrust, every strike came from stolen knowledge; how could she explain the Loa imprisoned in her soul. To make matters worse, the more time that passed, the more her mother's memories faded. Already her understanding of Aṣẹ had faded to a distant memory, and Vesper had to learn what she could through trial and error, often with disastrous results. Just last week she had set part of the villa on fire while making her supper, and this morning, while attempting to jump from her home to the village, she overshot, ending up deep in the wheat fields, unable to draw on any power for fear of what she would do to the crops if she took their energy. In the end she was forced to walk, grumbling under her breath at her stupidity. Fighting was easier, though, as long as she didn't think too much, her body simply reacted, moving by reflex.

"This I understand," said Kehinde, turning down his lips while nodding to himself. "This is why we train so that the body has the will to defy its limits. Take some time, drink some water, and we— Vesper!"

Kehinde rushed to her side as a shooting pain shot through her skull, gasps of agony pouring from her throat. As if just thinking about her called the Loa, Lillith attacked the walls of her prison, her titanic blows growing with each passing moment, sending jagged spikes of hurt through Vesper's skull. "I'm fine," she said with a shuddering breath, leaning against Kehinde, grateful for his strong presence.

"Perhaps we've pushed too hard today," he said, holding her up. "You are only human, no matter what your abilities."

"I think—yes, that might help," said Vesper, pushing, using all of her will to hold shut the door to Lillith's prison. The Loa had been silent for the last few months, so much so that Vesper had let her guard down, hardly noticing that she was there anymore. But now her mother saw an opportunity and was doing everything she could to break free. Using Kehinde's arm to steady herself, Vesper shifted her vision, following the glowing threads of power that flowed in all directions. With a deep breath she drew on the well of power that flowed from the low bushes and shrubs that were scattered around the training area, using the vegetation's life force to reenforce the barrier of Lillith's prison, once again muting her to a distant buzz.

"Come, I will take you home," said Kehinde, taking her training spear and hooping it through a sling on his back. "And I will make sure that you eat this time... and go to sleep."

"The nightmares come when I sleep," she said, shivering despite the heat. "I can get a few hours here and there, but I end up waking in a cold sweat each time, terrified and alone in the dark." Kehinde shook his head, his long, gray braids falling over his face. The old warrior knew some of what had happened that night, but not all of it, and Vesper didn't care to tell her tale fully. If she were honest with herself, she wanted nothing more than to leave what had happened in the past and never talk about it again.

"I know it is your family home, but you should not be in that house by yourself," he said as they set down the road in the flickering twilight.

"I'll be fine," said Vesper. "My father has promised to return and spend the winter. "It will be better with him here and not at the emperor's side."

"Your father spends too much time coddling that old man. With Magda gone, he should be here with you, with us."

Vesper smiled to herself, memories of a young, strong Marcus Aurelius in the bath fluttering through her head. It was strange: Lillith's memories of her time with the emperor were the strongest, often coming to the surface without warning. "That old man is wise and kind. He is lucky to have my father, but my father is lucky to have him. They make an excellent team, and the empire thrives under his rule."

"How could you know such things," asked the tall warrior, frowning down at her.

She looked away quickly, her eyes focusing on the fading remnants of the setting sun. She had to be careful. Her mother's memories of the emperor often floated to the forefront of her mind at the strangest times, and even without knowing the man, she had a strange affection for him, with the thought of him now making her blush. "My father talks of him when he comes home. And I have read letters he sent to me... his words were always kind."

"Romans are good for nothing," spat Kehinde, "regardless of their station."

WIth a laugh she leaned against his wiry frame, comforted by his presence while they walked on in silence. They were almost back to the villa when Vesper tensed, knowing something was wrong. "No one is supposed to be here," she said, pushing away from him. "Could it be Sandawei?" she said, an odd mix of anger and fear bubbling up from her stomach.

"No, Sandawei aren't much for riding, and there are horses around back. They don't seem to be trying to hide. Perhaps your father has returned."

Vesper nodded, the tension draining out of her shoulders as she strode with purpose to her home. Coming closer, a small contingent of men appeared from her aunt's garden, each of them wearing the silver armor of the legion, the tall plumes from their helmets making them appear taller than they were.

"Roman legionaries," said Kehinde, a predatory grin coming to his face. "Not the usual auxiliary fools we normally see. I have always wanted to try my hand against such men. To see if they live up to their reputation."

"We're about to find out," said Vesper as one of the legionaries broke from the group, cantering on a tall horse to meet them.

He came to a stop before them, holding tight his reins to control his horse who danced about nervously. "I am First Centurion Atticus, and my men and I have been ordered to escort you."

Vesper frowned up at the centurion in confusion, trying to make sense of his words. "Escort me where?" she said at last, backing away from the nervous horse.

The first centurion frowned at her, clearly not used to having his words questioned. "By ancient treaty as old as the empire, you have been ordered to fulfil your sacred duty and serve as the emperor's hand."

She shook her head in confusion, glancing over at the dozen or so men who appeared behind the first centurion guiding a smaller horse that was clearly meant for her. "I'm afraid you've made some sort of mistake," she began, trying to keep her voice calm. "My father serves as hand to Marcus Aurelius. I am far too—"

"Your father has been arrested for treason," he said, raising his chin.

"Treason! For what!" shouted Vesper, feeling like she'd just been struck by lightning.

"For the murder of the emperor, for the death of Marcus Aurelius!"

Vesper heard his words and staggered back, her breath coming in shallow gasps. What she was hearing was impossible. Her father was not capable of such things. He was a loyal servant even to the point of putting the good of the empire before that of his own family.

"He is to be executed ad gladium as part of the games to celebrate the new emperor."

"Games... new emperor," said Vesper, shaking off her stupor. "Who has been named?"

"It was the will of the emperor that his son rule, and so it has been done."

"Commodus, Commodus rules," she whispered as the blood rushed from her head. Vesper didn't remember falling, only the shock of hitting the earth. From her mother's memories she knew the son of

Marcus Aurelius well, and now that he ruled, she feared for the world.

The End.

ALSO BY RHETT GERVAIS

Apprentice: The Last Witch of Rome - Book One

Betrayed by an empire she was sworn to defend, enslaved by an emperor she was meant to protect.

At the dawn of the empire, the witch women of the Ose tribe looked to the future, and what they saw terrified them. To protect the world they made a pact with Augustus, Emperor of Rome. In return for destroying his enemies, he would allow a single Djambe to serve at his side, to use her magic to guard against the encroaching chaos they knew would one day come.

Vesper's destiny was to serve at the emperor's side, but when the mad Emperor Commodus comes to power, he doesn't believe in magic and old fairy tales. In a fit of rage, he destroys her people and orders her execution, just as a dark tide takes hold of Rome.

Now with the world in peril, Vesper must do the impossible, survive her execution and save an empire that has betrayed her.

Apprentice is the first in The Last Witch of Rome series. An exciting historical fantasy novel set at the height of the Roman Empire.

ABOUT THE AUTHOR

Rhett's love for all things science fiction grew out of a Sunday morning family tradition of watching Star Trek re-runs on the CBC. His love of storytelling is the result of too many hours as a dungeon master trying to murder his players!

He lives in Pincourt Canada with his wife, daughter, and a crazy calico named Maggie.

Made in the USA
Monee, IL
31 August 2020